KU-079-793

BIG thanks to:

Elizabeth Sacre for the encouragement; Nancy Miles for the support; and Leah McGrath and Clare Skeldon for being my first teen readers. Cheers, me dears, also to the Faber crew especially Julia Wells for her fab editorial input and for not going bonkersatronic when the manuscript was a teeny-weeny bit late.

Get Your Paws Off!

Rachel Wright used to live by a tropical beach in sunny Fiji. Now she lives by a railway track in south-east England. Something, somewhere clearly went wrong. She has written more than 40 children's non-fiction books and two novels including this one. When not busy writing, she says she spends her time going on country walks and having intelligent discussions with her mates. She is, of course, using the word 'intelligent' wrongly.

Get Your Paws Off! is Rachel's second book about Loz and Dex. The first, *You've Got Blackmail*, is also available.

C158014601

by the same author
You've Got Blackmail

Praise for *You've Got Blackmail*:

'*You've Got Blackmail* hits all the right notes – a riotous read that teenage girls will adore.' *Sunday Express*

'This is full of humour, with mystery after mystery ... It's a short book and a quick, fun read that moves at a manic pace ... *You've Got Blackmail* is a rocket full of fast-paced laughs that will keep you entertained all the way through.' Chicklish

'A very amusing and entertaining read.' Write Away

'This is a very funny book with some fantastic characters, especially Lozzie whose witty remarks and ingenious solutions to her problems make this a brilliant read.' Seven Stories

'Quirky, hilarious and brimful of wonderfully eccentric characters, is sure to tickle the sensibilities of upper primary and lower second secondary pupils.' ReadPlus

Get Your Paws Off!

Rachel Wright

faber and faber

First published in 2008
by Faber and Faber Limited
3 Queen Square London WC1N 3AU

Typeset by Faber and Faber Limited
Printed in England by CPI Bookmarque, Croydon

All rights reserved
© Rachel Wright

The right of Rachel Wright to be identified as author
of this work has been asserted in accordance with Section 77
of the Copyright, Designs and Patents Act 1988

*This book is sold subject to the condition
that it shall not, by way of trade or otherwise, be lent,
resold, hired out or otherwise circulated without the publisher's prior
consent in any form of binding or cover other than that in
which it is published and without a similar condition
including this condition being imposed on the
subsequent purchaser*

A CIP record for this book
is available from the British Library

ISBN 978-0-571-23531-5

2 4 6 8 10 9 7 5 3 1

Contents

1

The Nonsense Begins

'You *are* joking, aren't you?'

I am standing at my open front door, gawking like a goldfish. Dex, my best mate, is on the doorstep, a dog lead in one hand.

He groans: 'I'm really sorry about this, Loz, but Ed's only had Assassin for five days and he doesn't know the neighbourhood and Mum's going frantic.'

Assassin has got to be the ugliest mutt on the planet. He looks like the kind of dog a skinhead would have, and he was given to Ed (Dex's brother) for his eleventh birthday.

Dex groans on: 'He must've wandered off this afternoon while we all were out. Mum's discovered there's a hole in our garden hedge behind the shed. She's driving round Withingdean looking for him now. Dad's searching in Newlands Park. They want me and you to check out the streets and playing fields by the cemetery. What d'you say?'

I say, 'No way, dude. It's cold, it's nearly dark and I'm watching *South Park* on DVD.'

He goes all tight-lipped.

'Aw, c'mon,' I plead. 'Be reasonable. It's the episode where aliens plant a probe up Cartman's bum.'

Dex holds up his hand like the Buddha . . . only without the inner peace.

'It's OK,' he says stiffly. 'No need to explain. I understand.'

'You do?'

''Course. I'll be fine on my own. Absolutely fine. In the dark. Among the graves. With the living dead.'

Bloody Nora.

'If I need any assistance, I'm sure there'll be a helpful paedophile lurking in the shadows. Or perhaps a dog-friendly killer with a knife. Who knows, with any luck there'll be a coven of devil worshippers looking for a sacrifice who'll be only too glad to help me find Assassin in return for my torn-out heart.'

I go get my coat and a torch.

'Aw, thanks, Loz,' grins Dex when back I come, scowling. 'You're a pal, a true pal. You sure you don't mind?'

'Mind? What's to mind about paedophiles and devil worship?'

And with that, muttering, I follow Dex out into the darkening street.

It's gone seven-thirty by the time Mrs F (Dex's mum) phones to call off the search for the night. When Dex's ringtone blares out in the shadowy cemetery, we both shriek so loudly it's a wonder the dead don't tut.

'That's an hour and a half of DVD viewing I won't get back,' I grumble as we trudge homewards across the playing fields.

'Oh, shut up,' snaps Dex. 'At least you're not wearing glasses that are bust.'

In his hurry to escape from a ghostly white plastic bag, Dex had tripped over a tree root and broken the side of his specs.

'Look on the bright side,' I had said, trying to cheer him up. 'Maybe now your dad'll let you have contact lenses.'

'Yeah, right! And maybe he'll let me have acting lessons like I've been asking for all term.'

Mr F is not a reasonable man. According to him: 'Acting and drama is for poofs.'

By the time me and Dex reach civilisation – well, street lighting – I'm so hungry and fed up, my head could've fallen off and rolled into the gutter and I wouldn't have cared. Limping along Wilkinson Close, the two of us talk rubbish in different accents to cheer ourselves up. Dex does his French accent, which he thinks is *très, très bon* – he is *très, très* wrong. And I do my rather excellent impersonation of an Irish person who for some reason turns Australian. As we cut through to the High Street, Dex sings 'Who Let the Dogs Out?' in what starts as a German accent, and I glance up at a lamp post – and my eyes practically go *boinnnng* out of my head. There, tied on the post, about halfway up, is a colour poster of Assassin. Underneath his mean, menacing face, in black letters it says:

MISSING

**Brown and white mongrel called Assassin
Has a white belly, four white paws
and one ear half bitten off
Disapeered from
Park Crescent on Tuesday October 4**

£25 reward

No questions asked for safe return

Underneath that, there are two phone numbers: one is a mobile number, which I'm guessing is Ed's. The other is for The Diner, which is this fab, greasy-spoon kind of café with a jukebox that Dex's parents

4

run on the High Street, just a few doors down from my mum's hair salon.

'Blimey,' I gasp, looking at Dex. 'Your mum got that up quick.'

'It wasn't Mum,' he sighs. 'It was Ed. The second he clocked Assassin was missing he began designing a poster.'

My jaw drops to the pavement – *thud!*

'Are you telling me the whole time we've been faffing about in a pitch-black graveyard, Ed's been all cosy and snug at home on his computer?'

Dex nods heavily, like his head is made of concrete or something. 'He reckons Assassin's been dognapped.'

'*What?*'

'He doesn't believe he's lost. He reckons he's been deliberately nicked off the streets for a reward, and the sooner the reward is advertised, the sooner the dognapper will bring Assassin back.'

I do not believe it! 'Why would he think *that*?'

'Because he is a crime-obsessed mutant.'

This is a fact. Ed *is* a mutant. And crime-obsessed. Not long ago, Dex found him drawing up plans for taking our school hostage. And last summer he went around scanning rooftops for snipers, wearing a black woollen balaclava.

'Well,' I say, glancing back at the poster, 'whatever's happened, let's hope Assassin turns up soon.'

Dex makes a grunting noise. If he had a choice between living with a dog and not living with a dog, you wouldn't need to be Englebert Einstein to know what his choice would be.

Unlike our top mate Ems – who is so dog-doolally, you only have to mention the word 'puppy' and she turns to slush.

'Oh, poor Ed,' she gushes at school the next day. Dex has just filled her and the rest of the girls in on the latest riveting news. 'And poor Assassin.'

The five of us are sitting together in the cafeteria after lunch: me on one side of the table in between Tasha and Dex, Ems and Nat on the other.

Ems burbles on: 'Ed could be right, you know. Dognappers don't just target pedigree breeds . . .'

Tasha goes back to reading her magazine.

'If they see a mongrel wandering the streets, they'll snatch him to sell down the pub, or they'll wait till a poster goes up and claim the . . .'

'Anyone for a quiz?' tweets Tash, looking up from her copy of *Rebel*.

Open-mouthed, Nat, Dex and me eyeball her like crazy.

'What?' she goes, all innocence.

That girl is outrageous.

She reads aloud: '"Question one: If you could change one bit of your body, what would it be?"'

6

Rolling her eyes at Ems, Nat begins.

'I'd change my legs,' she says. 'They're like "Bird! Bird!"'

I add, 'I'd shrink everything from my waist to my knees.'

Dex goes, 'I'm short and skinny and my glasses are held together with tape, but apart from that I'm a stud.'

Which makes us crack up.

Tash turns to Ems. 'How about you, Emsie, what would you change?'

There is a pause. Then: 'Nothing, really. I'm OK with how I look.'

Tasha's finely plucked eyebrows practically shoot into space.

Recovering from her shock, Tash carries on: '"Question two: If you could have a super power, what would it be?"'

'Invisibility,' Nat says straightaway. 'That'd be *sooo* cool.'

I say, 'Being able to fly would be groovy.'

Dex goes, 'I'd be invincible.'

I've no idea what that means.

Ems adds, 'I'd like to be able to talk to animals, especially Ruby.'

Ruby is Ems's dog.

Tasha puts down her mag. 'If you're not gonna take this seriously, Emma . . .'

Ems goes to protest but Dex cuts her off.

'What super power would you choose then?' he says, leaning back in his chair, looking at Tash.

'Mind-reading. So I know what people are thinking about me.'

'D'you think that's wise?' This is Dex, with a grin.

Tash ignores him. '"Question three . . . If you could go back in time and change one thing, what would it be?"'

'Oh, that's easy,' grunts Nat, fiddling about with her fork. 'If I could go back in time, I'd go to the start of term and strangle Mrs Braithewaite.'

Mrs Braithewaite is our tutor for PSHE. For reasons best known only to herself and other dictators, she's decided our year – Year Ten – have to spend one afternoon a week 'helping out in the community'. Last Wednesday, Nat and Ems were cleaning graffiti off a bank.

'I'm telling you,' grumps Nat, splatting a bit of left-over casserole with her fork, 'there's only so many times you can hand a bank cashier a bag of currants and say, "Here are some currants for my current account."'

At that moment Old Retardo – Mr Leonardo, our head teacher – swoops into the cafeteria and goes straight to the front of the lunch queue. On his way out, sandwich and apple in hand, he passes our table and squints at Nat, a trace of a smile on his lips.

All at once Ems clutches her arm. 'OhmyGod-ohmyGod. Did you see? He knows it was you behind Operation Move Mini!'

Nat's face cracks into a grin. Last week she got her brother Michael and his rugby team mates to pick up Old Retardo's Mini and hide it in the rhododendron bushes.

'I've had a better idea, for when next we have Mrs Braithewaite in the IT suite,' she whispers, leaning in.

Her small freckly face is so lit up, you could guide a plane down with it.

'What? What're you going to do?' This is the rest of us, also leaning in, agog.

'You'll see,' she says, being tantalising and mysterious, which is no mean feat when you've got casserole sauce down your shirt. 'All I'm saying is, it'll *really* disrupt the lesson.'

Fan-bloody-tastic! Of all the lessons in the known galaxy, disrupted ones are my favourite.

2
Drama! Drama!

There's a furious outburst from the back of the auditorium: 'No, no, NO!' Brian leaps out of his foldaway director's chair and storms to the stage. He's so unbelievably aerated it's a wonder his glasses haven't steamed up.

'Gilbert, you're supposed to be playing a sixteenth-century *duke*,' he yells, 'not a ******* pantomime dame! And what are those ridiculous children at the back *doing*?'

Now, personally, I'd have thought it's obvious what me and Dex are doing. We're standing in for Servant One and Servant Two, who haven't turned up for rehearsal, and we're putting real effort into our roles. Dex has got two strips of foam inside his mouth to push out his lips like a trout, and I am wearing my sunnies and an excellent false nose. As I am to tell him later, after we've been banished from the stage, we wouldn't need to invent funny business

11

if *Twelfth Night* had some decent jokes. I mean, here's one of the play's top gags: 'Now is the woodcock near the gin.'

What in the name of Deirdre Barlow is hilarious about that? Even my sister Karen comes out with stuff less tragic than that – and she's part vampire, part goth.

Of course, I wouldn't be stranded in this pants-arse production if it weren't for Mrs Braithewaite and her stupid PSHE electives. When she announced at the start of term that me and Dex would be spending Wednesday afternoons doing Shakespeare with a bunch of unravelled people, I felt like shouting, 'Shoot me now, why don't you?'

Which, incidentally, is what Tasha did shout out.

But then she'd just been told she'd be digging a canal.

Dex, of course, practically did a tap dance when he heard he'd be doing his elective in a theatre. He nearly sang the whole of *The Sound of Music* when he managed to persuade Brian, the play's director, to give him a part in the show.

'I've had an idea about my role,' he burbles, after I've been ordered to make the tea and he's been told to prompt. 'I think I'm going to play him like Daniel Craig in *Casino Royale*. You know, intense but with a sensitive side . . .'

I interrupt: 'Dex . . . you are playing a bystander in a street. All you've got to do is stand and stare.'

He sighs like it's *me* being the plum.

'And do you think Daniel Craig would be where he is today, Lozzie, if he'd just stood and stared?'

'Are you going to be this poncy all afternoon, Dex?' I ask.

There is a pause. 'Yes.'

★ ★ ★

The kitchen is at the back of the building, overlooking a courtyard with a fishpond. Once inside, I bung the kettle on the stove and open the window to let in Onslow, the theatre's cat. Over the tannoy, I can hear Brian getting his wiggy-looking wig in a spin.

'Trevor, why are you walking like a duck? I don't care that you're not used to wearing tights. Right, boys and girls, once again, from the top. And Ronnie, perhaps this time you would be so good as to speak your own lines, not Desmond's!'

Onslow is now weaving in and out of my ankles like a maniac, shedding hairs all over my trousers, which is a delight.

I coo, 'OK, OK, your milk is coming,' and I am just about to open the fridge door when a familiar cheery voice booms in my ear, 'This is what you need!'

I yelp, Onslow squeaks and Bunty ('cause that's

who it is) sticks a bit of paper up on one of the cupboard doors.

Bunty plays Maria, one of the hysterically funny (not) characters in *Twelfth Night*. She's about fifty with mad, sticky-up, greyish hair, and she's really round, really short and really not normal. Like the other actors, she's in the show as part of some community care rehabilitation thingy (that's the technical term, I think). And on good days when she takes her pills properly, she's bubbly and chirpy, all chatty chat chat. This is one of her good days, fingers crossed.

'I've done a tea chart,' she beams, picking up Brian's special mug from the counter and cradling it to her massive chest.

Reluctantly, I go over and take a look.

'As you can see,' she booms, running a stubby finger down a list of the cast and crew (I must say, Bunty's nails are shockingly chewed), 'Brian takes only half a teaspoon of sugar in his tea; he's very careful about his weight; never eats biscuits or cakes or the like. Delilah likes her tea black without sugar; she's extremely careful about her diabetes. Lionel takes his tea *extra* strong. Be sure to leave the bag in the cup for fifteen minutes at least . . .'

'*Fifteen minutes!*' I interrupt. 'Blimey! You could tar a road with that!'

At this Bunty chortles so hard she ends up having a

coughing fit. I go and get her a glass of water, and as she's glugging it down Delilah looms into the kitchen.

Delilah does the costumes for *Twelfth Night*. She is also Brian's wife. She's tall. Really tall. As tall as my dad, with a long face like a horse; long hair, black and dead-straight; a severe fringe, and a huge nose. I've only seen her a few times before, and each time she was glaring down at someone – Brian mostly. Whenever she comes into a room it's like all the air has been sucked out. This time is no different. She says, her voice tight as tight:

'Bunty, you're wanted on stage.'

Like someone out of the Famous Five, Bunty cheers, 'Hurrah!' and bustles off, still clutching Brian's mug to her bazooms.

Delilah swivels her head to face me. Yikes!

'Is that a nose from Props you're wearing?' she asks.

My hand flies to my face. 'Oh ... yeah ... sorry. I –'

'Please return it to the prop room now.'

And just like that, she's gone, striding back the way she came, leaving me to scoot off to Props to return my latex conk.

I am still there half an hour later, checking myself out in an excellent moustache, when the fire alarm goes off.

3

Brian Goes Berserk

If Brian has a list of people he'd like to hit with a plank, my name is on it in capital letters and underlined twice.

'I bet Sir Kenneth bloody Branagh never had to contend with arson when he did his *Twelfth Night* at the National!' he rants out in the car park, as smoke pours from the kitchen window. 'You can be sure dear old Ken never had to direct a cast of mental misfits with evil black smoke billowing about!'

All around me the cast and backstage crew are glaring viciously at Brian and shivering slightly without their coats. In my ear, Dex is hissing, 'The 'tash, Loz, the 'tash!'

Quick as a wotsit, I rip off the moustache and shove it under my school sweatshirt.

'I'm really sorry about this, everyone,' I splurt.

Hey, how was I to know that a burnt-out kettle would create so much smoke?

Brian turns on me, pulling himself up to his full (short-arse) height. He's so pumped up with fury, I almost say, 'Do you need to let out some air?'

'Isn't it enough my beautiful theatre's up to its rafters in debt,' he explodes, 'without some teenage delinquent setting it alight?'

Teenage delinquent?

'The minute we get inside, I'm phoning your headmaster and having you taken off my production.'

At this, Dex's eyes go the size of ostrich eggs. I blurt, 'Wait, let me explain!'

'I'm not interested in your feeble explanations,' snaps back Brian.

'May I say something, please?' says Hattie, the theatre's stage manager.

Hattie steps forward and all at once the vein in Brian's neck stops throbbing – possibly because she is young, calm and beautiful, and her bosoms are level with his nose.

'Er, yes, Hattie, what is it?' he splutters.

In her silky voice, she explains how mad busy things are in Props, and how very much she'd appreciate it if he (Brian) would let me stay on to help her, under her strictest supervision of course.

For a moment Brian stares up at her like a total idiot, which he is. Then, getting a grip at last, he grumps,

'All right, yes, all right.'

I glance at Dex and make a face like 'Phew'. The punishment for getting kicked off an elective is scraping chewing gum off school property and naturally I'd rather hit myself over the head with a bit of lead piping than have to do that.

'So, what d'you want me to do?' I ask Hattie later, after the fire crew have gone.

The two of us are in Props, warming our bottoms on a radiator. We've already checked out the kitchen, which isn't too bad, if you don't count the eye-watering, throat-choking smell of smoke.

'I'd like you to take Eric for a walk,' she says, rooting around in her hippy-dippy bag for her van keys. 'He's been cooped up in the camper for an hour now, poor baby, and it'd be so lovely if he could have a run along the beach.'

Eric is Hattie's chocolate labrador. He's big and velvety and as loopy as a loon. On Monday, he chased Onslow up into the lighting rig. On Tuesday, he ate the key to Brian's front door. This morning he brought in all the fish from the courtyard pond. And as of this afternoon, he is banned from the building by order of:

1. Brian, who still hasn't had his front-door key back; and

2. Stan (the caretaker) who had only just restocked the pond.

In answer to Hattie, I say, 'Okay. Sure, no problem.' And next thing you know, her number is stored on my mobile in case of an emergency, and I'm out in the car park unlocking the bright yellow camper van's side door. No sooner has the door of the van slid open than the Loopy One hurtles out, his tail wagging so fast you could use it to whisk up an egg. Like a mad furry tornado he dashes round and round my feet then stops, stone-still, and looks up at me as if to say, 'C'mon then, are we going or what?' I can't help but laugh out loud. He really is the most bonkersatronic dog on the planet.

Still chuckling to myself, I clip on his lead and soon the two of us are trotting on our way: out of the car park, down Waterloo Street, over the busy main road and on to the wide promenade that runs alongside the pebbly beach. When we get to the bit of the prom near the bandstand, we cross over on to the beach and I unclip Eric's lead. Straightaway off he bounds, chasing after a seagull, while I stretch out in an abandoned deckchair, eyes shut, and daydream of Lee.

Lee is my boyfriend. *Yeeessss!* He's in Year Eleven, the year above me, and is lush, lush, LUSH. All the girls have a super-sized crush on him, and can you blame them? He's bloody GORGEOUS: tall and fit with dark, penetrating eyes and thick dark hair, ooh, yum, yum. Just thinking about him makes my insides fluttery. When he kisses me, it's like swoon, swoon – my legs turn to spaghetti.

Our first snog was at the end of last term, up in his bedroom. We were sitting on the floor, our backs against the bed, listening to a CD. He wriggled up close and slid one arm round my shoulders. Then leaning in, his lips practically touching mine, he whispered –

'Oi, is that your dog?'

My eyes snap open. '*What?*'

'I said, is that your dog?'

Standing in front of me is a red-faced policeman, jerking a thumb behind him in the direction of Eric.

Who is doing a poo.

The size of China.

Sticking out of the poo is a door key on a silver ring.

'Er, yeah, that's him,' I cringe.

Oh. Dear. Nelly.

The officer fires off some questions: 'Did you not read the sign saying dogs are strictly forbidden on this particular stretch of beach?' (No, I did not.) 'Will you please remember that in future and clear up the mess forthwith?' (Yes, I will.) 'Are you aware that forthwith means get on with it now?' (*STRESSSSSS!*)

Reaching into a pocket of my coat, I take out the plastic bag Hattie had given me and approach the monster turd.

Oh dear Nora! Ugh! Yuck! Could it *be* any more gross?

Wearing the bag like a glove, I pick out the key and wash it over and over in the sea. If this doesn't get me into Brian's good books I will kill him. And I'm not just saying that! Key clean, I then drop the stupid thing into my trouser pocket, and scooping up the poop, squealing, 'Eugh, eugh, eugh,' I chuck it in a bin.

After that, it's strict dog discipline all the way. I bark, 'ERIC, COME HERE,' and he chases another seagull. I yell, 'ERIC, COME HERE NOW,' and he licks his dangly bits. I screech, 'ERIC, DINNER-TIME,' and he gallops towards me. And before you can say, 'You great daft Muttley,' we're trotting across to the far end of the beach where the sign says it's OK for dogs to run free. Once there, again I do the lead-unclipping thing, and again Eric hares off – this time across the pebbles and out of sight, down the slope to the sea.

Now, as brilliant luck would have it, there's a kiosk close by. So, to pass the time usefully, I do what any normal person would do: I nip over and buy a KitKat and a cup of tea. I am just getting myself all comfortable on the beach, takeaway cup nestling in the pebbles by my side, thinking: *Maybe this elective malarkey isn't so bad*, when what happens? There's a burst of barking from down by the surf.

Bloody Nora! Can you believe it? I wouldn't mind so much but I haven't even got the wrapper off my bloomin' KitKat.

Leaping up, I scoot across the pebbles to where they start sloping to the sea. Far down by the surf, Eric is barking his head off at some man. I charge down the slope, shouting the Loopy One's name, and as I slow to a stop, the bloke's face comes into focus. It's Lee's dad, Dave Quick.

'Eric!' I yell for the squillionth time.

For the squillionth time he ignores me.

I grab his collar and tell him to 'Sssh'. Then to Dave Quick I say, 'I'm really sorry about that.'

All at once Dave Quick slaps on his wolf-like smile. I must say, for an older man he really is astoundingly fit-looking. It's no Agatha Christie mystery to me where Lee gets his dishiness from.

'Your dog doesn't seem to like me, Loz,' he laughs, holding out a warning finger to Eric. 'Must be my aftershave, eh?'

Smiling like a numpty, I explain how Eric isn't

actually my dog and how I'm minding him as part of my elective. Dave Quick nods, still smiling, and asks a few casual questions, like how's school, how's life, how are things with Lee and me.

'And how's your mum?' he says, last of all.

'Er, fine.' I look at my feet, not sure what else to say.

And can you wonder given that this is the reason: at the start of the summer Dave Quick and my mum dated for a bit. Yes, *really!* 'You'll be in therapy for months, Loz,' Tasha had said. Then suddenly Mum broke things off. Why, she wouldn't say. All I know is, she told her mate Man-Mad Marge that he was 'not all he seemed'. (I couldn't hear any more than that listening at the keyhole.) When I asked Lee if he knew what had gone on, he said no, but Mum was better off out of it – Lee doesn't get on with his dad. When I asked Mum if I should break up with Lee because of her and Dave Quick, she said, 'No, love. Of course not. I'm fine.' So I didn't.

Anyhoo. Still at the beach . . .

Dave Quick goes, 'Well, I'd better be getting back to work.' He is a painter and decorator. 'I only stopped for a walk en route to my lock-up.' He rivets Eric with a glare. 'You'd do well to keep that dog on a lead, Loz.'

And so saying, off he strides, up the beach, without a backward glance, leaving me to give the Loopy One a strict, strict talking-to before the both of us trot back the way we came: along the promenade, over the busy main road, up Waterloo Street, through the car park and over to Hattie's beat-up, rusty old VW camper van.

Which Eric gleefully refuses to go anywhere near.

'Right, that's it!' I fume, wrapping his lead tightly round my knuckles. 'Bad dog! Bad dog! I'm handing you back to Hat.'

But when I get inside the arts centre, there's no sign of Hattie anywhere. She's not in Props or in Wardrobe or behind the scenes at the back of the stage. I am just thinking where to look next when suddenly there's a roar of laughter from in front of the scenery. I pad over to the wings to take a look, and there, stretched out on a couch centre-stage is Onslow, surrounded by some of the cast.

One whiff of his furry playmate and that's it: the Loopy One is off – taking me with him. The cast scream. Onslow streaks upstage. And I only just manage to duck as Eric shoots through a fireplace in the back-stage wall.

'Now that is what I call an entrance!' announces Dex much later, on the bus home.

By the time he and the cast had leapt to my rescue, I was lying face down on the floor, Eric licking my ear.

'Look at it this way,' he burbles as I check out my

cuts and grazes. 'At least your week can't get any worse.'

I narrow my eyes at him. 'You think?'

'How could it?'

How spectacularly wrong can one lad be?

4
Chicken Fillets Are Go!

You know how the very old are always claiming your schooldays are the best of your life? Well, if this is true, all I can say is, there's not much point in me carrying on. All day Thursday I wait in a state of high tension for Old Retardo to give me a rollicking about the Eric scenery-destroying fiasco, but he doesn't summon me to his office. Instead I get a detention from The Blob – Miss Owen – for having an ink fight, even though it wasn't me who started it. Then I wait again on tenterhooks all day Friday, sure I'm going to be kicked off my elective, but again Old Retardo doesn't call out my name. On Saturday morning I find out why when my ringtone blasts. It's Dex. He begins,

'Loz. Me. Listen, want to hear some good news ...?'

I butt in, 'What's that crashing and banging about in the background?'

'I'll tell you in a sec, but first listen – I've got good news.'

'Go on.'

'You're not getting kicked off our elective!'

'*Really?* How come?'

'You know how Brian wasn't actually in the auditorium when you and Eric trashed his set?'

This is a fact. He was outside in the Portakabin doing a spot of emergency meditation.

'Well, when he got back, the cast said a stray dog had got into the building and wrecked the scenery. Your name was never mentioned!'

I cannot believe it. I am totally stunned. I had no idea the cast liked me so much.

'I had no idea the cast liked me so much!'

Dex howls with laughter then stutters to a stop. 'Oh, yeah – no, er, 'course the cast like you – well, those who know who you are. It's just they hate Brian more, and you and your disasters wind him up.'

I'm about to protest that the Eric fandango was not my fault when there's a hollow howl from the other end of the phone.

'Bloody Nora, what was that?' I gasp.

Dex lowers his voice. 'It's Bunty. I'm at the theatre and there's been a bit of an upset.'

'What kind of upset?'

'She overheard Brian saying something really harsh.'

'Like what?'

28

'Like she looks like an egg on legs.'

'Oh Nelly!'

'Exactly. She's taken a handful of her pills and washed them down with a can of Red Bull. Now she's running around the theatre with a sword, which may or may not be a prop.'

Yikes. 'So, what are you doing?'

'I'm hiding under the stage.'

'Where are the actors?'

'They're under the stage with me.'

'Brian too?'

'Dunno where he is. Jerry barricaded the under-stage door before he could get in.'

Nice.

Jerry plays Duke Orsino in the show. He's young, pale and twitchy – a geography teacher off work with stress – and on his arm there's a tattoo that says: *I am the Antichrist*.

I carry on, 'So, what's the plan?'

Dex loves a plan!

'We're gonna stay where we are till Bunty gets tired and falls asleep.'

'Then what?'

'Then we're gonna bundle her into Robin's car so he can drive her home, then the others are gonna carry on rehearsing and I'm gonna stay on for a bit before going to The Diner. Wanna come?'

I nod, which is helpful seeing as how we're on the phone. Then I say:

'Great, but first I've got to pick up that cake Mum ordered from Le Patisserie for Nana's lunch tomorrow.'

For reasons I can only put down to spectacular insanity, Mum has invited Lee to join me, her, Nana and Karen (my eighteen-year-old sister) for Sunday lunch to celebrate Nana's birthday. She's also invited Karen's boyfriend Dave, who smokes a lot of wacky baccy (cannabis) and once told Mum he thought he was an elf.

Back to the arrangements . . .

'Okay,' says Dex in answer to that bit about Le Patisserie. 'Let's meet at The Diner at twelve.'

Just then there is another hollow howl from his end of the phone.

I say, 'Want to make that half past twelve?'

He goes, 'Yeah, half twelve would be better. We'll meet at half past.'

But when I get to The Diner at quarter to one on the dot, Dex isn't anywhere to be seen. Mrs F spots me hovering in the doorway and beetles over, drying her hands on her apron.

'I haven't got any free tables, luvvie,' she splurts. The Diner is beehive-busy. 'You'll have to share with Ed.'

Smiling on the outside, but on the inside screaming, 'Take me now, sweet Lord,' I follow her over to the booth furthest from the door, near the enormous jukebox, where the mutant one is sitting in his brown anorak, trying on a pair of night-vision goggles.

For his birthday, Ed had asked for some night-vision goggles, a miniature digital video recorder and a bugging device for listening in to people via your mobile phone. His parents gave him the goggles and Assassin, who they got from a rescue centre. Dex bought him a can of deodorant for men.

Shrugging off my jacket, I slide on to the high-backed bench opposite Ed and nod hello. He takes off the goggles and gives me his usual dead-fish stare.

'What'll it be, luvvie?' Mrs F asks, glancing around the café to check on her paying customers.

I say, 'Some chips, please.'

She says, 'Fine.'

I say, 'Thanks.'

And just as she is putting her notepad back in her apron pouch, she blurts, 'Oh, you haven't heard, have you, Loz? Assassin's been found! We've had a call. A young man spotted him wandering up by the cemetery and is bringing him here any minute. Ed's waiting for him now.'

I beam. 'That's fantastic news, Mrs F. Brilliant! You must be really relieved.' Then, after she's scuttled off to the kitchen, I say to Ed, 'You must be really pleased too, right?'

Wrong.

'You may be pleased, Lauren,' he says in his weirdy, flat, robot-like voice, 'but I don't appreciate being a victim of crime.'

Good grief!

'This dognapper may think he has got away with it, but the last laugh will not be his.'

I almost say, he won't be having any laugh at all when he meets you, you fruit loop.

At that moment into the café comes a long, skinny, pointy-faced bloke, who looks about twenty, wearing a black Armani hooded top with a paint mark on the sleeve, black jeans and scuffed-up Reebok trainers. In his arms he's holding Assassin, who looks a bit sad and thin.

Straightaway, Ed slinks up to The Hood. The Hood makes a face like 'What the . . . ?', Ed does his zombie stare and Assassin goes berserk with excitement. He leaps out of The Hood's arms, jumps up at Ed and runs round him in circles, knocking over a chair with his tail. Then he jumps up at Ed again, just to check he is who he is, and when Mrs F come shooting out of the kitchen he jumps up at her, too.

From then on, it's a bit like one of those funny farce kind of plays where characters keep going in and out of doors: Dex strolls into the café, clocks the situation and exits into the kitchen; Mr F comes out of the kitchen, hands over the reward dosh and goes back to his cooking; Mrs F says thanks to The Hood and she and Dex go out back; The Hood ruffles Assassin's head (he's *sooo* not impressed) and skedaddles out the door.

All the while this is going on, Ed watches The Hood, eyes staring like a cat. As soon as Mrs F and Dex have gone out back, he puts on his balaclava and follows his 'suspect' on to the street, Assassin at his heels.

'You do know Ed is tailing that hoodie bloke, don't you?' I say to Dex when at last he joins me from the kitchen.

Dex plonks two plates of sausage and chips on the table. I love Mrs F.

'Probably wants to see where he lives so he can assassinate him later,' he gruffs, taking off his jacket.

Dex flops down on the bench opposite me and spears a sausage on to his fork.

'Is it just me,' I say, picking up a couple of chips, 'or is Ed now beyond deranged?'

Dex bites into his sausage. 'It's not you. Ever since he tackled that mugger, he thinks he's the neighbourhood vigilante or something.'

During the summer a masked man jumped out at Ed from behind a bush and demanded his mobile phone. Ed refused and when the mugger swung at him, he ducked and karate-chopped his attacker's nose. The attacker ran off and Ed got his photo and his story in our local paper, the *Echo*. Mr F practically blew up with puff and pride at the heroic doings of his favourite son. Even to this day, poor Dex has to put up with seeing that photo of Ed in his tough-guy pose and karate suit plastered all over their house.

Dex rumbles on, 'He's turned his room into a detective's office, you know. On his wall he's got a map of the neighbourhood – or "his manor" as he calls it – with pins marking the places where he reckons he's seen suspicious stuff. On his desk there are these box files with newspaper cuttings about local real-life crimes. Last time I crept up behind him on his computer, there was a photo of Mrs Pipe from number sixteen on the screen with the caption: "Steals from supermarkets, question mark". Honestly, Loz, I'm asking you, how much more retarded can he get?'

While Dex is growling away I shake a splodge of ketchup on to my chips.

'Ooh, that reminds me,' he blurts, glancing at the red splat. 'When we were under the stage, Hattie said she used to do the props on *Casualty*. Guess how she made fake blood for the show.'

'Dunno.'

'By mixing gelatine, water, glycerine and red food colouring.'

'Woo!'

'I know! Guess how she made realistic-looking vomit.'

'Dunno.'

'By mixing tinned chicken soup and crushed Weetabix.'

I grin at Dex and he grins at me.

'So, what was the rest of the under-stage goss?' I ask.

He hoovers up some more of his chips. 'There wasn't much. Hattie said Bunty's list-making mania has now reached global proportions. D'you know last week she made a complete inventory of every single thing under the stage including a box of matches smothered in dust?'

I say, 'Do you remember that time me and you went under the stage and something scurried across your foot and you ran out screaming, "Help! Help! Help me! Help!"?'

Dex shoots me a look, the kind that would make concrete crack. I crack up laughing, and Mrs F beetles over.

'Do you two want a quick cup of tea?' she says, smiling at one of her regulars who has just walked in.

I beam, 'Yes, please.'

Dex goes, 'Please, Mum, thanks.'

And before you can say, 'I love Mrs F from the bottom of my heart', she's back with a lovely jubbly cuppa in each hand.

At practically the exact same time, me and Dex reach for the sugar bowl at the end of the table ... and stop.

'How come we've got brown sugar?' This is Dex. Stunned.

'Muffets recalled their white sugar from shop shelves yesterday,' Mrs F replies. 'When I went to Londis to buy another brand, only brown was left.'

Dex looks at the brown granules in the bowl as if they were rabbit droppings. He *so* doesn't do health food.

'How come Muffets recalled their sugar?' he says.

'A young man was rushed to hospital after adding poisoned sugar to his tea. The police don't know how the sugar came to be poisoned, so Muffets have recalled all their white sugar from shops as a precaution.'

From a nearby table Mrs F picks up a copy of that day's *Echo* and hands it over so that Dex and me can read the latest. Underneath the heading:

RAT POISON VICTIM RECOVERING

it says:

A 17-year-old youth admitted to Queen Alexandra Hospital on Thursday with Trithium poisoning is making a good recovery.

Trithium is a tasteless, odourless, white crystalline poison that is used to kill rats. In this case, the Trithium had been added to a 1kg bag of Muffets white sugar found at the youth's home.

When swallowed, Trithium causes patchy hair loss and sudden extreme lethargy, followed by a coma that can end in death.

'This young man is very fortunate that his mother got him to hospital before the poison had done irreparable damage to his internal organs,' said hospital toxicologist Ivor Girdle.

Out of the corner of my eye, I can see Dex's shoulders shaking.

Mine are starting to go, too.

'*Ivor Girdle?!*' he howls. I laugh so hard tea snorts out of my nose. 'What kind of a ning-nong name is that?'

We're still laughing like crackpots – about silly names we've made up (Dex is Dwain Dwopp; I'm Iona Bott) – when Mrs F scoots over to tell Dex his dad needs a hand out back.

'Ooh, maxi fun!' he mutters, dragging himself to his feet. Then, looking wistfully at me: 'What're you doing this afternoon?'

'Watching Lee play football.'

He blinks like a frog. 'Why?'

'I like football.'

This is a lie, obviously. A couple of Saturdays ago I sat through over two hours of Albion versus Man

United on the TV with Lee. When the commentator announced the game would go into extra time, I sent Mum a suicide text.

Shaking his head in disbelief, Dex collects up our dirty plates while I put on my coat.

'Have fun at the game,' he calls out sarkily as I walk to the door.

But, weirdly enough, I *do* have fun at the game – well, for part of it, anyway – because when I get to the pitch Tasha is there, cheering on her boyfriend Darren, who's in Year Twelve, the year above Lee.

'Hey,' I beam, nudging up beside her. 'I didn't expect to see you here. I thought your dad had grounded you for eternity.'

'Yeah, he had. But when he came downstairs this morning he was in such a good mood, I put on my most pitiful face and said, "*Please* can I go out?" and he said yes.'

'Excellent! Result! So, how come he was in such a top mood?'

'I think he and Mum had just been . . . you know.'

'Doing-the-do?'

Tash makes a face like she's swallowed Toilet Duck. 'It's not natural.'

She's not wrong there. No, really, she is not!

Desperate to stop any images of unnaturalness popping into my brain, I focus my eyeballs on Lee.

Honestly, could he *be* any more tasty? As I'm goggling him tearing down the pitch, Tash turns full frontal to face me and whispers,

'D'you notice anything about me that's different?'

'Er . . .' I stand back and check out her long, straight, dark-brown hair, perfect make-up and trendy clothes. Today she's wearing a short sweater dress over leggings and biker boots, and a cool leather jacket, undone. 'No. Why?'

She takes off the jacket and turns to the side. 'How about now?'

'Bloody Nora! Tash . . . what've you done to your bazooms?'

She glances from side to side to check none of the Year Twelve girls next to us is earwigging and leans in. 'I've put those chicken fillet things down my bra.'

'How *many*?'

'Six – three in each cup. What d'you think?'

'I think you need to take out four!'

She gives me a look that says, *Are you mad?* 'I think it really suits me being this big. Promise you won't tell anyone about the padding?'

I'm about to say, 'D'you think I'll need to?' when a humungous cheer goes up from the crowd: Darren has scored. Go, Darren!

Like on *Match of the Day*, he runs up the pitch, arms stretched out in victory, milking it for all he's worth, which really makes me and Tash laugh. Then, drawing level with us, he blows a massive two-handed kiss . . . and Felicity Bagnall from Year Twelve blows him a girlie one back; her big green eyes batting so hard, you can practically feel a draught.

That does it. Tasha launches straight into orbit.

'Did you *see* that?' she hisses. 'Did you see?' In between hisses she's giving Felicity the evils. 'She better bloody not be here to make a move on Darren. She better bloody not be after him.'

I tell her, 'Relax, calm down.' It does no good; her face is so red, she could go undercover as a tomato. 'You know what an outrageous flirt Felicity is. Anyway, Darren would never chuck you for her. She's probably here for one of the other lads. When the game's over, I'll ask Lee.'

But, as it turns out, I don't ask Lee that or anything else after the game because not long before the final whistle goes, my phone rings. It's Ems.

Sounding tiny and shaky and lost.

'Emsie, what is it?' I go. 'What's the matter? What's up?'

'It's Ruby,' she says, trying to steady the wobble in her voice. 'S-s-she's gone.'

5
Lost and Hound

Ems lives a fifteen-minute bus ride from our school, up near the golf course, in the posh bit of town. From her upstairs back bedroom window, you can see a massive garden, then fields, then woods. From my upstairs back bedroom window you can see a patch of grass, then a shed, then an alley. By the time me and Tasha get to her place, her dad is out searching the woods, and Ems, Nat and someone else I don't know are dotted about the fields, yelling Ruby's name.

Mrs Hodgson (Ems's mum) takes me and Tash through the house and out into the garden to the back gate.

'One of us probably didn't close this properly,' she says, opening the gate, 'and Ruby nosed her way out.'

Tash and me nod politely like *Yeah, that must've been what happened*, then leg it across the field to Ems.

One look at her tight, white face and my heart lurches.

'Oh, Emsie,' I cry, putting my arms around her. 'We'll find Ruby.'

''Course we will,' soothes Tash.

But we don't. And decades later, after we've all staggered indoors exhausted for tea and cake ('Home-made cake!' Tash is to tell Dex on Monday), Mrs Hodgson announces that she's going to report Ruby missing to all local dog wardens, animal rescue centres and the police.

By lunchtime the next day (Sunday) there are five hundred Missing Dog posters up across Sussex, which is the county where we all live. Each poster has got a photograph of Ruby looking like a show dog at the top, and underneath the words:

LOST

Weimaraner bitch called Ruby
Missing from a back garden in Hardington Villas,
Hove, since Saturday October 8

£200 offered for information
leading to her safe return

Tel: 0789 281 3147

As I am to explain to Nat and Tash late that night on MSN, I would have helped with putting up the posters, but when I told Mum where I was going, she said, 'Oh no, you're not! It's Nana's birthday lunch in a couple of hours and you've got chores to do.' She also said some other stuff such as, 'How many more times do I have to tell you to empty your pockets before putting your clothes in the wash?' but I don't share that nugget with the girls.

By the time Karen's boyfriend Dave lumbers to the door, all my chores are finished except for the upstairs hoovering. The reason I didn't have time to finish the hoovering is that halfway through the dusting, I had to fend off an attack by Karen. Honestly, goths are so *touchy*. All I said when she came downstairs in her pale foundation and panda black eye make-up was, 'Blimey! It's Death in a dress.' Which I thought was extremely amusing until she started beating me senseless with a cushion.

Anyhoo. Not long after the Morticia Addams incident, Dave turns up, then Nana. When I open the front door to Dave, he flashes his sexy, laid-back smile and trips over the step. (Dave has the face of a hunk and the brain of a brick.) When I open the door to Nana, she cries, 'Come here, me little darlin'' and crushes my ribs with a hug. Nana has the grip of a boa constrictor and a southern Irish accent. She's tiny: thin as a thread, short as a gnome. You don't need to be wearing jam-jar specs to suss my womanly bottom and hips don't come from her.

I beam, 'Happy birthday, Nana. I like your outfit.'

Today she is wearing a Barbie-pink velvety track-suit with lipstick to match.

'Brazen, isn't it?' she says with a wink. Then, later on, talking to Mum, she adds, '£6.99 from Primark, would ye believe?' And Mum replies, 'Yes, I would.'

The five of us are in the kitchen – Mum about to serve up – when the doorbell goes again. Like a heat-seeking missile on heat, I shoot off to answer it. One look at Lee standing on the doorstep in his low-slung black jeans, white T-shirt and black biker's jacket and ooh, er, yum. Talk about DEE-*lish*!

'Hey, babe,' he drawls, smiling like a hungry shark.

'Hey, sweetie,' I coo, grinning madly like a twit.

If only the lovers in *Twelfth Night* had dialogue like this!

He slips a hand round my waist and kisses me soft-ly on the lips. Swoon. Mercifully, it looks like he's got over my leaving the match early, which is a big relief. When I'd rung to explain, he'd been a bit huffy; said my going early had made him look bad in front of his mates. How daffy daft is that?

Walking in, he takes off his jacket, chucks it over the post at the foot of the stairs and sniffs the air.

'Your mum's doing roast lamb, yeah?' he grins.

'Yeah. There's roast potatoes *and* Yorkshire pudding, too.'

44

'Excellent. I'm like really starving.'

And with that, off we go to the kitchen, hand in hand, me thinking: *Please, please, God let Karen have been abducted by aliens.*

'So *this* is Lauren's fella!' beams Nana, as we come through the door.

Mum says briskly, 'Hello, Lee. Nice to see you again. Sit yourself down.' She points to the empty chair with a plate of roast lamb in front of it. 'Let me introduce everyone. This is my mother, Kathleen; this is Loz's sister, Karen; and this is Karen's boyfriend, Dave.'

At each introduction Lee smiles hello like he means it. He says 'Happy Birthday' to Nana, too.

'Lauren's got herself a good-lookin' charmer there, hasn't she, Karen?' grins Nana with a wink.

Karen smiles back. Tightly.

Yeeesss! For once in her life she's not the only one with fit-looking crush. Ha, ha, ha, ha, ha!

'Well, isn't this grand!' exclaims Nana, once we're all sat down. 'Both my granddaughters having lunch with their fellas.' She beams at Lee. 'Lauren tells me yer parents are divorced, darlin', and ye and yer father live on your own. Perhaps you could do him a favour and introduce him to my Anne here?'

All at once, me, Lee and Karen go as pink as prawns and stare at our plates.

Mum snaps, 'Do you mind!' and shoots Nana a daggers look. Then: 'How are you getting on with your driving lessons, Dave?' she says calm as cream, doing one of her speedy scene changes. 'Have you got a date for your test?'

Dave looks up from his plate, which is a first! 'Er, yeah, I, uh, did it yesterday.'

'Oh!' This is Mum. 'I didn't realise. How did you get on?'

'OK . . . 'cept for at the end when I drove into the side of a skip.'

Across the table Karen shoots me a look that says, *Leave it*; Lee grins to say, *I'm lovin' this!* Only Nana doesn't glare or grin or glug back a bucketload of wine. Instead she picks her handbag off the floor and plonks it on her lap.

'What ye need, young David,' she announces, opening the bag and rootling about, 'is a decent driving instructor. It took me a few tries before I passed my test . . .'

Thirty-nine to be exact.

'But Miklos got me there in the end. His number's in here somewhere. Give him a call and tell him Katty sent ye. He should be over that little nervous breakdown by now.'

She tips her bag upside down on the table and out comes all her stuff: her purse, make-up, comb, keys, scraps of paper, mints, condoms, glasses case . . .

Condoms?

CONDOMS!

OH. MY. GOD!

For a moment me, Mum, Karen, Dave and Lee sit staring at the condoms like goldfish that have just been told they've won a year's supply of tights. Then Karen makes a noise like she's gargling blancmange and Mum leaps to her feet.

'Karen! Lozzie!' She's scooping up plates like a mad thing. 'Time for birthday cake! Now!'

In seconds, the table is stripped barer than a bare baby's bottom. The three of us girls huddle round the sink.

I hiss, 'Mum! Did you see? You must've seen. Nana's having sex!'

And smiling like a saint, Mum says, 'Loz, please . . . don't put it into words.'

★ ★ ★

After lunch, up in my room with Lee, I flop down on to the bed.

'Well, that was monumental, with the emphasis on the mental.'

He laughs and flops down beside me.

After Nana had blown out the candles on her cake, Mum said, 'What did you wish for?' and she said, 'A

Harley Davidson.' Then over coffee, she announced that she's dating a hottie called Henry who still has his own hair and teeth.

'Your nan's sound,' grins Lee, rolling on to his side to face me.

'Yeah, she is, isn't she?' I grin back. 'Mad as a banana but sound!'

He laughs and at the exact same time there's a familiar bleep from a back pocket of his jeans. He checks his moby's screen, grins his shark grin, says, 'That can wait,' and leaning over me, puts his phone on my nightstand. That done, he then whips *my* phone out of *my* back pocket, switches it off and puts that on the nightstand too, before pulling me towards him.

Ten minutes of outstanding snogging later, Mum shouts up the stairs.

'Loz. It's Emma. On the phone.'

Unpuckering my lips, I shout, 'Tell her I'll call her back in a minute.'

As I say it, Lee does this totally dreamy thing with his tongue in my ear. (It sounds gross but it is *so* not!) Next thing, there's a knock at my door.

I DO NOT BELIEVE IT!

Fuming like a fuming thing, I roll off the bed and open the door a crack.

On the other side stands Mum, looking all concerned.

'I think you should call Emma back now, Loz,' she says. 'She's in a dreadful state.'

'Why? What's happened? Is it about Ruby?'

Mum nods. 'A man has sent a text message to say he's taken her and he wants £1,000, not the £200 on offer. Emma's father is refusing point-blank to pay up.'

6

Oh, Sugar!

I don't know what Lee is thinking, obviously, but my guess is it's not: *Marvellous — another date kippered by a dog!* When I switch on my moby to speed-dial Ems, he mutters, 'I don't believe this!' And when I try to stop him from nuzzling my neck while I'm listening down the line, he sulks.

'I'm sorry, sweetie,' I say, at last getting off the phone, 'but she's stressing really badly. The dognapper must've sussed her parents are rich so he's demanded more money, and now her mum and dad are arguing about whether to pay up. I couldn't've just not called her back, could I?'

Barely glancing up from his texting, he grumps, 'S'pose not.' Then, getting off the bed, he says, 'Look, Loz, I'm gonna push off now. I've got stuff I need to do. I'll call yer later, yeah?'

My insides droop. I want to blurt, 'No, no, stay, stay,' but of course I don't because:

51

1. It's obvious he wants to be off (clue one: he's already practically out of my bedroom door); and
2. I don't want him thinking I'm becoming one of those clingy, clingy girlfriends who hate to let their bloke out of sight.

So what I say is, 'OK. Cool. Call me later though, yeah – promise?'

And after he's gone, I feel all desperate inside.

★ ★ ★

At the bus stop next morning, Dex peers at the dark circles underneath my eyes.

'Blimey, Loz! Didn't Karen have any make-up or something you could've nicked?'

I tell him to shut up and swipe a swig from his carton of Ribena.

It's only eight-fifteen a.m. and already I'm shattered. A few hours after Lee had gone I began wondering why he hadn't phoned – that, plus the Ems situation, kept me stressing until I nodded off. Then at the crack of dawn I woke up with a jolt – no idea why – and started stressing again. That did it: I couldn't get back to sleep.

'Why didn't you ring *him*?' says Dex after I've given the blow-by-blow about Lee.

'How could I? He said he'd ring me, so I had to wait, *right*?'

Dex shakes his head like he thinks I'm deranged.

'Would it have killed him to have shown some sympathy for Ems?' he says, after a bit.

'Lee doesn't like dogs so he probably doesn't know how major this is for Ems.'

On the inside I'm wriggling here; I know Dex has a point.

He scoffs, '*I* don't like dogs but I can imagine how having your beloved pet held to ransom might be slightly upsetting.'

After about a century of Dex staring into the distance and me pretending to read the bus timetable, the number 52 pulls up. We shuffle on board and as we're swaying down the aisle, I spot a copy of the *Echo* on the floor . . . and practically keel over with astonishment. Staring up from the front page is Brian, *SMILING*. Talk about a bombshell! Who would have thought he could?

I snatch up the paper to show it to Dex and that's when the headline practically leaps off the page at us:

MAN IN RAT POISON COMA

Quicker than a wotsit, we're sat down and stuck into the front-page article. This is what it says:

A 57-year-old man was admitted to Queen Alexandra Hospital yesterday morning with Trithium poisoning. Brian Archer, who owns the city's Mermaid

Theatre, lapsed into a coma after drinking a poisoned cup of tea. The poison has been traced to a 1kg bag of Muffets white sugar found at his home. Two similar bags of sugar also found at the property were not contaminated.

Dex's eyes widen to flying-saucer proportions. 'Bl-o-o-d-y Nora!' This is us both.

We carry on reading. The story goes on to explain more stuff about the case, such as:

1. How the poisoner had left no fingerprints or tool marks on the sugar bags; and
2. How neither Brian or Delilah would have noticed the patchy hair loss side-effect because Brian wears a wig.

The story also features a long interview with Delilah about how Brian came to get poisoned. In a nutshell, this is what she says happened: On Sunday morning, Brian made himself a cup of tea sweetened with half a teaspoon of sugar, as per usual. Soon after, Delilah went shopping for the day, and while she was out, their decorator turned up – a young bloke called Ryan Bentley. This Ryan rang the bell and, getting no answer, let himself in with his spare key. (Apparently he'd told Brian he'd be coming round on Sunday, but

Brian had forgotten to tell Delilah.) When he got inside, he found Brian collapsed in bed, too weak to move. With the help of a neighbour, he carried Brian into his van and sped him to hospital. Tragically, Brian lapsed into unconsciousness just as the van was pulling up outside A&E.

'B-l-i-mey,' I breathe, dragging my eyes from the paper.

There is no reply from Dex.

'Blimey,' I repeat louder, right in his ear.

He yelps, then nods, then stares gloomily out of the window.

'I do hope this doesn't mean *Twelfth Night* gets cancelled,' he says, after a bit.

Good grief!

'If you're hoping for a career with the Samaritans, Dex, I'd forget it.'

★ ★ ★

Believe it or not, Dex is *still* rumbling on about *Twelfth Fright* when we get into school. Up ahead, over by the bike sheds, I can see Tasha pointing her 'chicken fillets' at Darren. ('I confronted him about Felicity,' she is to tell me later, 'and he says he'd never get off with her in a million years; she's way too bitchy and tarty.') Also by the bike sheds, I can see Nat, with her arm around a shrunken Ems.

'C'mon,' I say to Dex, tilting my head in their direction.

But no sooner have we started to go across than I hear a familiar voice calling my name. I spin round and there, luscious as life, is Lee. He says, 'Hey, baby,' and gives me a hug, which is nice. It would have been nicer if Dex hadn't been muttering '*Baby?*' in my ear, but I make a wide-eyed face at him and, getting the hint, off he scoots to comfort Ems.

Lee runs a finger down my sleeve. 'Sorry 'bout yesterday, babe.'

I huff, 'You promised you'd call.'

'I know. Something came up.'

'Like what?'

He glances at his shoes. 'Like, uh, Dad needed help. With this big job he's got on.'

'I thought he'd taken on an assistant to help him with his work.'

'He has. It's just, uh, his assistant refuses to work Sundays.'

I huff again, 'Well, you could've texted, you know!'

'Yeah, sorry. I—I forgot my phone.'

By now first bell has gone and there's the usual mad excited rush indoors. (I'm using the words 'mad', 'excited' and 'rush' wrongly.) As we lag along the downstairs corridor, Lee gives me these playful little nudges; I act like I'm not bothered. Then, coming to a stop, he grins and cries:

'Aw, c'mon, babe, you're killing me here. How about I come round yours tomorrow after eight to watch a DVD?'

I beam like a numpty. Note to brain: *Stop doing that*.

'All right,' I say, 'but only if I get to choose the film.'

Lee acts like he's been stabbed in the heart.

'Aaargh . . . please, nothing girlie, I beg.'

Which is odd, because in the whole eight weeks we've been going out (not counting the summer holidays when he was in Spain seeing his mum) I've never picked a soppy film. Not once.

Our DVD date agreed, Lee sprints off to wherever he is going, and I slope into maths. Which is the usual riot of joy and delight . . . not. I mean, what in the name of Nora does $2x + 3y - 4x^2$ mean when it's at home? And why does Mr Murphy keep insisting that quadratic equations are fun? Does 'fun' mean something completely different in his language – like 'tall' means 'small' in Starbucks?

To pass the time more sensibly, I send Ems a note. It says: *Wnt 2 cum bowlin L8R?*

But she doesn't write back. She doesn't even nod her head at me. She just stares emptily down the row in my direction before sagging back over her desk.

Eventually Mr Murphy drags himself away from the party in his head and comes up to her.

'Are you feeling unwell, Emma?' he asks gently.

She looks up at him, face all grey.

He tries again. 'Are you not well, Emma?'

Tash gives her a nudge and from the row behind, Megan McGrath calls out, 'Please, sir, her dog got nicked at the weekend. There's posters up an' every-thin'.'

'Oh, I'm sorry to hear that,' says Mr M kindly, like he means it. 'I hope you'll be reunited very soon.'

But as Dex whispers to me once Mr M has gone back to the mathematical rave in his head, 'How likely is that?'

Not very is the answer.

On Sunday evening Mr Hodgson had said to Ems, 'Your mother and I have had a discussion and we've agreed that giving dognappers money only con-tributes to their cruel trade. This is a matter for the police.' But as Ems had sobbed down the phone to me straight after, 'What good are the police? When Mum first told them Ruby was missing, d'you know they didn't even give her a crime reference number until she insisted on having one? It's obvious they're not bothered about finding Ruby. Not now they've got a sugar poisoner on the loose.'

'She has got a point, you know,' I say to Nat after school. The two of us are walking through the parade of shops to Nat's bus stop – her to catch the bus to her house full of mad brothers, me to the bowling alley to meet my dad. 'The police aren't gonna make finding Ruby a top priority with this sugar poisoning business going on, are they? Particularly not here, in the centre of town, with all the other major crimes they've got to sort.'

Nat nods wisely like an old professor. Like an old professor with short brown hair that looks like it's exploding from her head.

I sputter on, 'If only her dad would just cough up the ransom. I mean, I know he reckons if they pay up now and the dognapper gets off free, there's nothing to stop him from nicking Ruby again, but even so. Can't he see how the stress of this is ruining Emsie?'

Again Nat does her wise old professor nodding routine. Then: 'Oooh! Wait up!' she splurts, and turns to go into the Co-op.

'Er, how come you're going in there?' I ask.

'To stock up on sardines,' she says.

'Why?'

'I've got my reasons.' She's smiling mysteriously.

'Are they sane reasons?'

'Is the Pope lactose-intolerant?'

'Uh, dunno. Is he?'

'I've no idea. I thought you might know, being a Catholic.'

'Nat . . . tell me truthfully . . . are you on pills?'

While Mad Sardine Woman is stocking up on mystery supplies, I wander round the shop to the bit where the magazines are kept. Scanning the racks, I spot the front-page headline on the evening edition of the *Echo*:

TRITHIUM FOUND IN 5 MORE SUGAR BAGS

Pouncing on the paper, I do a speedy skim-read. Turns out, five of the bags of sugar recalled from shops by Muffets have been found to have rat poison in them. *And* all seven contaminated bags, including Brian's and the first victim's, came from shop shelves in *Sussex*. The police have now declared a product-tampering scare.

'What is a product-tampering scare exactly?' I ask Dad later, after we've changed into our stylish (not) bowling shoes.

For reasons I can only put down to colour blindness, Dad is once again wearing his neon-orange bowling shirt. I have told him that with his shaved head and that shirt he looks like a giant baked bean, but will he listen?

'What it means, my little Lozenge,' he says in reply to my question, 'is that someone has gone into various supermarkets, nicked seven bags of sugar, taken them home, adulterated the contents with rat poison then put them back on shop shelves.'

'But why? Why would anyone wanna do something as evil as that?'

'Oh, there could be lots of reasons.' Dad is now keying our names into the console at our lane. 'The culprit could be a terrorist looking to publicise his cause; he could be an extortionist looking to make money from Muffets; he could be a whack job. Those are the usual suspects.'

By now Dad has selected a ball from the rack and is marking his run up to the electronic line. To the right of us, there's a bunch of lagered-up lads, swearing and mucking about. Next to them are Felicity Bagnall and her mate Melanie Tate, and two other girls I don't know.

Dad runs up to the line. He swings the ball and just as he's about to let it go I have a thought.

'Hang on –'

He tries to stop his throw. Too late. Down the bowling lane he flies, hand stuck to the ball.

All at once the lager lads whoop and howl; Felicity and Melanie look at Dad as if to say *Em-barrass-ment!* Dad picks himself up and stalks back up the lane.

'Lozzie,' he whispers, really cross, 'are we bowling or not?'

'We are. Sorry. It's just you said, "Those are the

usual suspects." You mean this tampering thing has happened before?'

Dad drills me with a death-ray stare. It's the same look he gave Nana last Christmas after she lit a fag next to Mum's brandy-soaked cake and the whole thing went up in flames.

He sucks in a breath. 'Yes, product tampering has happened before. Yes, that's why most foods, except sugar it would seem, come in tamper-proof packaging. OK? Case closed? Can we bowl?'

Smiling weaker than a weedy weakling, I nod. And so the match begins: Dad playing like a pro from start to last, me bowling like a cabbage pretty much throughout.

'Possibly not your finest hour, my little Loz,' he reflects as the final scores flash up on the board: 200 points to DAD, 60 to LOZENGE. He squeezes the top of my arm. 'Pity, you got off to a cracking start.'

And I did. I was doing bloody brilliantly until I heard Felicity Bagnall laughing her stupid, squeaky laugh, and, turning to look, saw her and Melanie Tate giving me and Dad the subtle (not) once-over. When I looked a second time they were doing it *again*, eyeing me in a sneery, superior kind of way.

Dad gives me one of his hefty squeezes as we go to change out of our tragic shoes.

'So, what's it to be this time?' he says, nodding at

the café area. 'Pizza? Burger? Double chips?'

'Actually, Dad, I'm not really that hungry.'

He feels my forehead like I'm sick.

'It's not like you to forego food designed to clog up your arteries,' he says.

'I know. It's just, uh, I don't feel much like eating right now.'

And honestly, who can blame me? As we left our lane, Felicity Bitchy-Knickers once again laughed her stupid, squeaky-toy laugh. And when I turned to give her my worst look, I caught Melanie Tate sniggering something about me behind her freakishly large hand.

7

Chicken Soup and Fake Puke

School the next morning is the usual pile of pants and nonsense . . . only ten times worse because poor Ems is in such a state. All through break she's like a miserable, washed-out shadow following us girls about. Over lunch, she takes one look at her egg salad sandwich and bursts into tears.

'Th-th-the police still haven't traced the moby the d-d-dognapper used to send the ransom text,' she sobs, sucking in big gulps of air.

Tash puts an arm around her, and from one sleeve Nat pulls out an avalanche of tissues and pushes them across the table to Ems.

'They say it'll take weeks to trace the number.' Ems is dabbing away at her eyes. 'But how can that be? Don't they know if they don't find her soon, the dog-napper will sell her at a private auction? Don't they know if she goes to auction I will never see her again?'

Across the table, Nat and Tash swap worried looks. I can tell they're desperately rummaging through their brains, like me, searching for something hopeful to say, but what? What *can* we say? Not even what happens after lunch boosts Ems up, and since what happens after lunch is possibly the most brilliant thing Nat has ever done in a history of doing brilliant things, it just goes to show how crushed Ems is. This is what Nat did:

Before school, somehow (don't ask me how) she got Mental Michael (the caretaker) to let her into the IT suite. There, she slipped a truckload of sardines inside the covers of the overhead lights and turned the lights on. By lunchtime the stink was rank. No one could work out where it was coming from. By two o'clock, the stink was beyond rank. So much so that when we all shambled up for our double period at the computers with Mrs Braithewaite, she had no choice but to cancel the lesson and let us off early because there were no other rooms free.

'That girl is a genius!' Tasha cries, as practically the whole class sets off for an educational trip to the arcade.

'That girl is a genius!' I cry later in The Diner to Dex. 'Someone should put her on a podium and turn her into a god. Prince Philip has been made into a god by a tribe in the South Pacific and Nat is *way* more brilliant than him.'

If Dex is impressed by my knowledge of the life and times of Prince Philip, or by anything else I've said since we waved goodbye to Ems at the arcade, he doesn't show it. Like in an exam, he just sits staring out of The Diner's huge window, chin in hand.

I lean across the table and squeeze his elbow. 'You OK, dude?'

He nods without shifting his gaze.

'What's up?'

Silence.

I drop my voice. 'Is it your hair?'

His head snaps round. 'What's wrong with my hair?'

'Nothing!'

'You said Surfer Blond is a great colour.'

'It *is*!'

If you're a surfer with a tan.

I'm about to say, 'If it's not your hair, what *are* you thinking then?' when Mrs F trolleys up and plonks two bacon sarnies on the table. Honestly, if there were a Premier League for mothers, Dex's mum would be right at the top, only a couple of points behind mine.

'Now, don't be all afternoon eating these,' she says firmly. Me and Dex assure her we won't. And after she's tootled off with the usual reminder: 'Remember you two've got homework to do,' Dex leans in.

'S'pose Ed is right.'

'You *what?*'

'S'pose Assassin wasn't just lost and found.'

'Oh, be sensible!'

'No, listen. S'pose he was dognapped for the reward as Ed claims.'

'But I thought we'd agreed Ed was barking up the wrong tree with all that dognapping paranoia rubbish?' I hear what I've just said and laugh. 'Barking up the wrong tree . . . dogs barking, get it?' Dex's face doesn't crack. 'Oh, please yourself.'

He steams on: 'Think about it, Loz. When Ed came up with his dognapping theory, no one believed him because (1) there was no proof a dognapper was about, and (2) Ed is a cretin.'

So far, so medically accurate.

'But now we know for a fact there *is* a dognapper about, maybe he was right.'

Hmm. 'OK . . .' This is me, speaking slowly, waiting for my brain to boot up. '*Sooo* —?'

'So — if Assassin was dognapped, he must've been dognapped by The Hood, yeah, because that's who returned him. And since it's way too massive a coincidence there are two dognappers in the neighbourhood, it must've been The Hood who dognapped Ruby!'

My brain has a nippy riffle through the facts.

'All righty,' I say, thinking, thinking, 'but Ruby and Assassin are really different kinds of dog: she's a beautiful pedigree worth seven hundred quid; he's got a head shaped like an anvil . . .'

Dex cuts me off. 'I know, but remember what Ems said after Assassin went missing.'

'No.'

'She said dognappers don't only target pure breeds. They're just as likely to bundle a mongrel into their van to sell down the pub or to hand back in return for a reward. I was checking this out on the internet last night and she's right. Dognappers nick different dogs for different reasons. Sometimes they even round up street dogs to use as bait in illegal dog fights.'

'*Really?* Oh God! That's horrible!'

Dex leans in closer, all keeny keen keen. 'Say Ed did tail The Hood on Saturday . . .'

Which I'd bet my last Jaffa Cake he did.

'He'll have made notes about where The Hood went and what he did and stuff like that, yeah? If The Hood went home, I reckon Ed'll have his address filed away for future surveillance. If I can get that address, what d'you say we go by the place, just to see if we can spot Ruby in the garden or something?'

My brain is now going off in a zillion and one directions like a pinball machine. 'Hold on! If The Hood *is* a dognapper, he'll have had dogs at his place that Ed will've seen. How come Ed hasn't gone to the police?'

'Maybe The Hood was in between dogs when Ed tailed him. Maybe he only snatches one dog at a time. Ruby wasn't taken until about four o'clock on Saturday afternoon, remember? Assassin was returned at around one.'

It's about now that Mrs F looms up to our table, demanding to know what's wrong with our sandwiches, and do we think she's got nothing better to do than make food that no one wants to eat?

Right away me and Dex start to chew. Chew chew, gobble gobble, chew chew. By the time she's finishing up her rant with 'Go home now, the pair of you, to your own homes, mind, and get on with your homework,' our coats are on, our heads are down and we're practically out the door.

Back on the High Street, walking past Woolworths (ooh, pick 'n' mix half price!) I say, 'OK, s'pose Ed has got The Hood's address on his computer or in a file – how are you gonna get it off him? If he's still suspicious about The Hood and has got him under surveillance, he's never gonna share his findings with you in case you muscle in on his investigation. And if he isn't still suspicious about The Hood and you ask for his address, he'll know something's up and he'll start tailing you.'

Dex nods heavily. Who better than *he* knows the seriously warped ways of Ed?

'I've thought of that, and that is why I have come up with a plan.'

'What kind of a plan?'

'A well-worked-out one.'

There is a pause. Quite a long one actually.

'Dex . . . are you going to tell me this plan or am I going to have to give you a Chinese burn?'

He tells me the plan.

'Tomorrow morning while everyone's out, I'm going to search Ed's room and hack into his computer to see if he's got a file on The Hood.'

'Excellent thinking. But won't you need his password to get into his computer?'

'Yes, thank you, Nancy Drew, I will, which is why I shall be searching his room first. Mind you, I've already got a pretty good idea what it'll be.'

'But how are you gonna wangle the day off school to do that?'

'Oh, I won't be skiving the whole day. There's *Twelfth Night* rehearsal in the afternoon, remember.'

Remember? How could I possibly forget? My big toe is still killing me from this morning when Dex jumped on it for joy after Old Retardo had told us the show has a new director.

'OK,' I say, getting back to business, 'so how are you gonna bunk off all morning? Your mum'll never believe you're ill.'

'She will if she finds a splat of realistic-looking puke by my bed. Now, all I need is a packet of Weetabix and a couple of tins of chicken soup. Any chance you could lend me a fiver?'

8

The Name's Bones . . . Sherlock Bones

That night I watch a DVD up in my room with Lee, all safe and snug in his arms. Next morning the lovely, warm, cosy feelings I have inside vanish as Karen stomps into the kitchen.

'You better've emptied your pockets this time,' she snarls, pointing her beaky nose at the washing machine I'm loading. 'If there's even a hint of white tissue on my stuff, you're dead.'

I tell her to shut up. She doesn't. She bangs around toasting Pop-Tarts. And after she's gone – to drink chicken blood or whatever it is she does – I unload the drum and from my laundry's pockets remove three crumpled-up tissues, one KitKat wrapper and one door key on a silver ring.

Looking down at the door key, I feel a little tug of sadness inside. It's so weird to think of Brian in a coma instead of at the theatre swearing and yelling; so weird to think of him lying on his deathbed instead of storming about in his wiggy-looking wig. I am still thinking back – wondering if Karen had the last Pop-Tart – when Mum shouts, 'Loz, your bus leaves in one minute!' And yelling 'STREEESSS!' at the top of my voice, I drop Brian's door key into my coat pocket, throw on my coat and fling myself out the door.

Now naturally, under normal circs, me and Dex would let the girls in on our plan to rescue Ruby. However, we've agreed not to say anything this time in case Dex can't find The Hood's address and Emsie gets let down. *Sooo* . . . when I get into school I tell them he is off sick with a migraine.

'Probably caused by that Surfer Blond hair dye,' shouts Nat, opening a packet of Cheesy Wotsits.

The two of us are sitting together, surrounded by chatter, waiting for English to start.

'You can get brain cancer from hair dye,' Tash chirps from behind.

Ems leaps in. 'Is that true? I've never heard that before. Can you really get cancer from dyeing your hair?'

Me and Nat twist round in our chairs to stare at her, eyebrows up. This is the first time she has actually joined in a conversation since Ruby got nicked.

Tash nods wisely. 'Oh yeah! Hair dye is a killer. It can give you a brain tumour for sure.'

'Only if you drink it, you numpty,' says Nat, who has inserted two Wotsits up her nostrils, to excellent comic effect.

Just then Miss McKinley, our English teacher, stalks into the classroom and yells, 'Quiet!' about twenty zillion times.

Still facing the back, I say softly to Ems, 'So . . . no developments on the Ruby front then?'

She goes a bit pink and wriggly: 'No, no.' Then, pretending to look at her York Notes: 'I'd tell you if there was.'

Hmm.

After a busy morning spent eyeing Ems closely and counting my teeth with my tongue, I wolf down a ham and mustard sandwich and shoot off to *Twelfth Night* to check in with Dex. He's bound to be in the prompt corner, er, prompting, so I head for the side of the stage. Dashing along one of the backstage corridors, I glance into Wardrobe, stop, backtrack and look again. Desmond (who plays Malvolio) is standing in the middle of the room with his back to me, wearing nothing but fishnet stockings with yellow tights underneath and a black leather thong.

I say a quick prayer: 'Please, please, God, let that have something to do with the play,' then leg it again. Past Props, round the corner and slap bang into Bunty. *Ooof!*

'Don't tell me you've started another fire?' she says cheerily in her foghorn voice.

Honestly, you set light to one measly old kettle.

I splutter, 'No. Sorry . . . are you all right?'

'Of course I am, you silly sausage.'

From the folds of her ginormous knitted skirt (*knitted?*), she pulls out a bit of card.

'I've done you a copy of Brian's address,' she announces grandly, like she's just invented the sandwich toaster or something.

I take the card from her outstretched hand, thinking: *What fresh list-making madness is this?*

'He regained consciousness this morning,' she adds.

'*Really?* Wow. I didn't know!'

'Oh yes! With any luck he'll be home at the weekend. I thought you and young Dexter might like to send him a card to mark the occasion.'

Er, can you get cards that say 'For You – Now You Are Out Of Your Coma'?

Bunty bubbles on: 'I've included his home phone number in case you want to pop round for a visit.'

Inside my head, I grin like a muppet. Imagine Brian's face if the first home visitor he gets after returning from the brink of death is me! Outside my head, I go, 'Thanks, Bunty. Thanks a lot.' And so saying, I slip the card into my coat pocket alongside my phone.

Just then Hattie nips round the corner, on her way to the loo, I guess.

'There you are, Lozzie!' she beams. 'I could do with another pair of hands in Props, so if you want to make you, me and Bunty a quick cup of tea, I'll meet you in there in a minute. Bunty, are you rejoining me?'

Bunty nods yes; Hat says, 'Great'; I go, 'Don't you want me to take Eric out for a walk?'; and Hattie replies, 'No need. He's being minded today by my girlfriend, Megan.'

Girlfriend?!

I can feel my cheeks going red. I tell myself: *Be cool, Loz. Be jet-set. Don't say anything retarded.*

'Oh, right . . . your girlfriend, yeah.'

Leave it. Leave it. Let it lie.

'I know a Megan, but she isn't a lesbian.'

WALK AWAY FROM THE AREA!

OhGodGodGod!

Cringing, *cringing* on the inside, I ponder my options en route to the kitchen:

1. I could wet my hand and stick it in the toaster.
2. I could put my head in the oven and turn on the gas.

As truly excellent luck would have it (NOT), when I get to the kitchen Delilah is there, glowering out the window. At what, it's hard to say. There's nothing happening outside. Maybe she's just caught sight of her reflection in the glass.

I know I've said this before, but she really is *mannish*-looking. And tall. *Freakishly* tall. I wonder if Dex is right and she truly is a bloke in drag?

'Hi, Delilah,' I say brightly, quickly adding, 'It's good news about Brian, yeah?'

For a moment she stares at me blankly in a way that almost makes me shiver. Then, getting a grip, she replies, 'Er, yes. Yes, it is.'

Out of politeness, I chirp, 'Would you like a cup of tea?'

She goes, 'What? Er, please.'

And so saying, out she swoops, without so much as a 'tatty-bye', adding, 'I'll be in Wardrobe when you're ready.'

Still reeling from the thrill of *that* riveting conversation, I get out the teabags, mugs and sugar (not Muffets, thank the Lord). Above my head, Bunty's smoke-stained tea chart is stuck to the cupboard door. Over the tannoy, someone – Brian's stand-in? – is saying, 'Lionel, I don't think Sir Andrew would break-dance halfway through that speech, do you?'

Getting on with my slavey-slavey-no-wages chore, I flick the kettle's switch (*now* they get one that clicks itself off!), check out Bunty's chart and make four mugs of tea. Then, like in an egg and spoon race, I hurry along to Wardrobe with one of the mugs held out in front of my chest. On the way, in the corridor, I pass Desmond gliding along, still wearing the yellow tights, fishnets and thong.

The thong has metal studs on the pouchy bit.

Good grief!

'Greetings, Lauren,' he says in his rich, actory voice.

'Greetings, Desmond,' I say. Note to brain: *Do not stare south at the pouch*. 'D'you know if Dex is still prompting?'

'No. He's now on stage standing in for Olive. She's had to pop out to see her psychiatrist.'

Of course.

One quick dash back to the kitchen later and I'm on my way to Props, hands full, carrying the other three mugs of tea. From outside the props room door I can hear Hattie and Bunty talking inside.

Hattie is saying, 'That young decorator is a hero.' Bunty agrees. 'If he hadn't got Brian to hospital so promptly, he may very well have died. The longer a Trithium-induced coma goes untreated, the more likely the victim is not to pull through. If he hadn't turned up at all, Brian would now be dead.'

I tap the door with my foot and a beaming Bunty lets me in. Hattie is sitting at the big central table, snipping leaf shapes out of green crêpe paper. Behind her are three tree-shaped wire frames propped up against the wall.

I plonk the mugs on the table and say, 'Sorry it took me so long.'

Hattie smiles and, jabbing her scissors in the direction of the wire trees, goes, 'We need enough leaves to cover those by tomorrow.'

Quick as a wotsit, I snatch up some scissors and, sitting next to Hat, join in the snipathon. By the time Dex pokes his head around the door – to announce Bunty is wanted in Wardrobe and Hattie is needed backstage – the props room table has enough paper leaves on it to make the Jolly Green Giant a coat. Like the crew of that ghost ship . . . the *Mary Whatsit* . . . *Mary Celeste* . . . everyone disappears – by everyone I mean Hattie, Bunty and Dex. And by the time Dex comes back, there are enough cut-out leaf shapes to make the Jolly Green Giant a three-man tent.

Dex plants both hands on the table, facing me, and leans in.

'Guess what I saw backstage just now?' he grins.

'What?'

'Desmond stuffing his thong with a pair of socks!'

'Good grief! I hope St John's Ambulance are standing by on opening night in case any women in the audience faint.'

Chuckling away, Dex sits down opposite me, and

suddenly remembering, I blurt, 'Ooh, wanna hear some gossip?'

'Always.'

'Hattie's gay.'

'*No!*'

'Yeah.'

I fill him in on the detail – i.e. Hat's girlfriend's name is Megan. Then, moving swiftly along: 'So . . . what d'you find out this morning? Did you search Ed's room? Did you hack into his computer?'

Dex leans across the table and lowers his voice. Why? There's no one else about.

'Yeah, I got into his computer. You'll never guess where he hides all his passwords and stuff. In a note-book in his pants drawer. I ask you! What kind of a lentil brain hides a code in with his pants? Anyway, as I could have predicted, his password *is* "Assassin". Like no one who knows him could've worked *that* out . . .'

'Dex?'

'Yeah?'

'Any chance you could get a shifty on *vis à vis* the point?'

'Oh, yeah, right. Well . . . I got into his computer and found a folder called "Surveillance" but I couldn't read anything in it because it was all in code.'

'Oh . . . so you mean there were no entries saying, "1.15: Put on tragic balaclava and followed suspect

81

out of Diner. 1.30: Tailed suspect in tragic balaclava to his house"?'

'No.'

'So you never got The Hood's address?'

'Oh yeah, I got his address. It was on a scrap of paper in a box file on Ed's desk. I also found something else in that box file.'

From a pocket of his trousers Dex pulls out a large folded piece of paper and hands it over. 'Here, have a look.'

Carefully, I unfold the bit of paper, which looks like a poster, and have a read. At the top it says:

ACE DOG DETECTIVE AGENCY

And underneath:

Expert in finding all dogs,
especially dognapped ones taken for ransom.
You get your dog back. I sort the bloke out.
No questions asked.

Email: ed@killthepresident.co.uk

IMMEDIATE ANSWER
Open every day after 3.30 p.m. except Monday
because I have karate.
Open all day Saturday and Sunday.

I look up at Dex. Gobsmacked. 'This is a wind-up, right?'

He shakes his head. 'And that's not the worst bit. Wait till you hear the rest.'

'What?'

'He's got himself a client.'

'*No!*'

'*Yeah!* Someone has emailed him to say they've seen his advertisement on some DogMissing website and would like to employ him to get back their dog. Does this address ring any alarm bells: ems.hodgson@ virgin.co.uk?'

My jaw smacks the table – *clunk!*

I DO NOT BELIEVE IT!

Ems has teamed up with Sherlock Bones.

9

What Would Scooby Do?

According to the case files of Sherlock Bones, The Hood lives up near the golf course, not far from Ems.

'*Where* exactly near the golf course?' I puff as Dex does his power walk routine from the theatre to the bus stop.

How a boy whose life's mission is to do no sport whatsoever manages to walk so fast is a total mystery.

'He lives on Anderton Avenue. Number fourteen.'

Anderton Avenue? Number fourteen? A light switches on in my brain. From out of my coat pocket I pull the address card Bunty had given me and take a look. 'Fourteen Anderton Avenue? That's where Brian and Delilah live!'

Dex stops and for a moment we stare at each other like doughnuts that have unexpectedly been dunked.

'That doesn't make sense,' he says quietly, after a bit. 'Unless . . .'

'Unless what?'

'Unless . . . The Hood is Brian and Delilah's son.'

'Huh? I've never heard any mention of a son.'

'Me neither, but what does that prove? Up until today you didn't know Hattie was gay and you actually *chat* with her.'

'OK,' I say slowly, brain booting up, 'but if The Hood is their son and he keeps the dogs at home, they must know about his dognapping, yeah?'

There is a pause while Dex has a think. 'Maybe they are in on it.'

'Oh, *behave* yourself!'

'Why not? You got to admit, there is something Cruella de Vil-like about Delilah . . .'

Well . . . now you mention it.

'And they need money to keep the theatre going. I overheard Brian saying he'd never have agreed to direct "this bunch of inadequate amateurs" if the theatre weren't in trouble. Remember what he said out in the car park after your one-woman production of *The Towering Inferno*?'

'No.'

'About the theatre being up to its rafters in debt?'

'Oh . . . *yeah*.' Hmm.

It's gone four-thirty by the time Dex and me get to 14 Anderton Avenue. On the bus over, we'd discussed surveillance tactics and come up with an ingenious plan. This is it:

1. We wander casually round the outside of house, beadies peeled, to see if there's a way to look into the back garden. If we can't peer in . . .
2. We ring the doorbell and ask The Hood would he like his car washed or something. (He'll have to let us inside to fill up a bucket, so we'll be able to see into the back garden and check whether Ruby is there.)

Now brilliantly, as it turns out, the house is one of those Victorian ones with an alley behind that runs between Anderton Avenue's back gardens and those in the next street. When we get to the alley it's deserted – totally. Casual cool(ish), we stroll along, past the lines of tall wooden fences to the back of number fourteen . . . and freeze. From Delilah's back garden, there's barking. Deep barking. The kind of barking a big dog like Ruby would make.

All of a splutter, I call out her name: 'Ruby? Ruby?'

Dex drops down on one knee to give me a leg up. I step up on to his thigh and have nearly managed to steady myself enough to peer over the fence when a huge Rastafarian bloke appears in the door of the fence behind us.

'What do you think you're doing?' he shouts.

My heart practically rockets out of my chest.

'Er . . .' This is Dex, quivering.

'Er . . .' This is me, quivering too.

'Clear off. You've no business looking in other people's gardens. Go on. Clear off. Now.'

To the end of the alley Dex and me scram before the man's yelling brings other nosey neighbours running. So much for Mission Casual Cool.

'That could be Ruby back there!' I gasp as we burst on to the road.

Dex nods, face tight. 'Time for Plan Two.'

But when we ring number fourteen's front doorbell, nobody's home.

'All right,' murmurs Dex, his brain going whirr, click, beep, whirr. He grabs my arm. 'Time for Plan Three.'

'Plan Three? What's Plan Three?'

'Plan One but with the sound down. This time it's vital we do nothing to bring that Rasta bloke back out into the alley.'

But when we pop our heads round the top of the alley, Mr Rasta Bloke is still on the wrong side of his fence, can you believe! What *is* it with nosey-parker people like him? What is their problem? How are Dex and me ever supposed to crack serious crime with everyone constantly popping up and shouting, 'Clear off'?

Dex mutters, 'If only there was a way of getting through to the garden from the street.'

I shove my hands in my coat pockets as we limp

back round to the front of the house. And that's when it hits me: a brainwave of global proportions. 'We get into the garden through the house!'

From the way Dex is looking at me you'd think I'd just morphed into a pickled egg.

'How can we do that? The only way we can do that is if we break into the house and – Oh no. Oh no. The answer is no way. *No way!* Have you lost your *mind*? Do you know how hard it is to break into someone's house? You can't just toddle up and crowbar a window. You have to build up to it. You have to start small, nicking sweets and stuff from Woolworths. Then pinch a bike, do a bit of proper shoplifting, break into a car. You can't just . . .'

'Relax.' Blimey! 'Who said anything about breaking in?'

Dex throws his hands on his hips (yes, *really*!). 'How *else* are we going to get in through the house?'

Out of the pocket of my coat I pull Brian's front-door key on its silver ring. Slowly, like a hypnotist with a pendant, I swing it back and forth in front of Dex's nose.

'Imagine Ed's face when he sees the headline: LOCAL LAD CRACKS DOGNAPPING RING,' I say in a ponderous, mesmerising voice. 'Imagine how good your picture will look in the *Echo* next to Ed's in his karate suit.'

Dex's eyes are now gleaming so brightly, it's a wonder I'm not struck blind.

'Let's do it!' he goes, all fired up. 'Let's do it. Let's break in.'

Talk about a quick costume change! 'You sure?'

'Hey, what's the worst that can happen?'

'Six months in a youth offenders' centre?'

'Regular meals, no Ed, no Dad, TV. *Foof!* . . . How bad can it be?'

10
Splat! Splat!

My heart is thumping like the clappers as I slide
Brian's key into the lock. Wildly looking back and
forth over my shoulders, I push open the door and me
and Dex go in. We step straight into a huge lounge
that looks like it's only just been decorated: the pic-
tures have been taken off the spotless cream walls and
there's a strong pong of paint. Against the back wall of
the lounge there's a staircase. Opposite the front door
is an open door that leads to a kitchen. Dex nudges
my elbow, chin jerking at the open doorway, and,
hearts jumping, blood pumping, we creep, quiet as
cats, across the polished floor towards the kitchen.

Suddenly from upstairs a phone rings and we both
hit the ceiling – *splat! splat!*

'Bloody Nora!' croaks Dex, coming back down,
hugging his chest. My own heart has exploded like a
blown-up shed. 'Bl-o-o-dy hell!'

Shaking like caffeine freaks on a freak-out, we

switch our phones to Silent (ace thinking, Dex) and on tiptoes make our way into the kitchen and across to the half-glass back door. At first I'm so one hundred per cent sure we're about to find Ruby in the garden, my eyes can't believe what they are seeing. Then I hear my own voice gasp, '*It's an Alsatian!*'

Dex's face drops faster than fast.

'Maybe Ruby's upstairs, sedated or asleep,' he says, trying to sound hopeful.

But when we get upstairs we only find three empty rooms: a bathroom, a bedroom with a double bed, and a half-painted study. In a corner of the bedroom there's a sideboard covered with propped-up photos of Delilah and the Alsatian. In a corner of the study there are tins of emulsion, some decorator's overalls and a black Armani hooded top with a paint mark on the sleeve.

As I stare at the familiar black hooded top, a terrible thought jolts through my head. 'Oh. My. God!'

Dex looks up from what he's reading on the desk.

'We have made a *massive* mistake,' I say in a strangulated voice. 'The Hood doesn't *live* here. He *works* here! He's not Delilah's *son*. He's her *decorator*. He's the bloke who let himself in on Sunday and rushed Brian to hospital!'

Suddenly my legs are wobblier than a jelly belly. A feeling of dread crushes in on me from all sides.

Breaking into someone's house and uncovering definite proof they are a dognapper is one thing. But breaking in only to find the person you thought was a dognapper is, in fact, a bloke everyone is calling a hero . . .

'We've gotta get outta here, now!' I hiss.

In practically a single bound, I spring from the study to the top of the stairs. Right behind me is Dex, going, 'You know that thing I was reading . . .'

We are halfway down the staircase.

'It confirms a round-the-world cruise trip for Delilah . . .'

We're now on the bottom two steps.

'The booking was made on Sunday evening – the same day Brian went into a coma.'

I stop and look at him, stunned. But not for long, because at that very moment there are sounds from outside the front door. Someone rootling through a bag. A key going into the lock.

Oh Nelly!

Oh God!

My feet root to the spot.

11
Panic Stations Go

In the nick of time, Dex grabs my arm and yanks me headfirst into the nearest hiding place – a cupboard with slatted doors under the stairs. My heart is hammering so hard it's a wonder it doesn't burst through the slats and have someone's eye out. Through the gaps I can see Delilah walking into the lounge. For one mad minute I think about leaping out and screaming 'Aaargh!' in the hope she faints from shock, but then my brain thinks: *What if Dex faints, too?*

Delilah drops her bag and coat on to the big brown leather sofa on the opposite side of the lounge from the stairs and goes into the kitchen. By the slatted light coming through the cupboard door, I shoot Dex a panicky look. Should we make a dash for it? Have we got time? Too late. She's back. With the huge Alsatian not far behind.

Beside me, Dex is breathing jerkily like a maniac; I

can practically hear him sweating. Over by the sofa Delilah is getting some paper and a phone out of her bag. Monster Dog is roaming around, sniffing. Sniff sniff. Sniff sniff.

Please, please, don't let him come near the cupboard. Please, please ... Oh no. He's here. *He's snuffling along the bottom!*

Delilah settles herself on the sofa, phone to ear. Monster Dog whines and scratches at the cupboard door. My heart jumps into my throat. Glancing over her shoulder, Delilah barks, 'Be quiet, Tyrone.' Then into the phone: 'Oh, yes, hello ... I'd like to cancel a cruise booking I made ... Delilah Archer ... yes, 14 Anderton Avenue ... Yes, yes ... No ... no, some funds I was expecting didn't come through, that's all ... Yes ... Thank you. Good bye.'

By now Monster Dog is really trying to nose his way into the cupboard. Looking up from the sofa, Delilah goes, 'What is it, Tyrone?' I press my hands deep down into my coat pockets to stop them from shaking. My brain shrieks: *You have got to get her out of this room NOW.* But how?

And then it hits me, like a bucket of cold water to the face.

Of course!

OF COURSE!

Fast as a fury, I yank my moby and Brian's address

from my coat pocket and start dialling the number on the card. Tyrone barks. Dex squeaks. Delilah crosses over to the cupboard. I punch in the last digit. Nearer and nearer she comes. She reaches out for the door-knob. The phone in the study rings. There is a heart-paralysing pause. And she turns and hurries off upstairs, Tyrone at her heels.

YEEEEEEEEEESSSSSSSSSSS!

Thank God.

Thank you, God!

Thank you, thank you, thank you!

Like greyhounds out of a trap, Dex and me burst from the cupboard. My size fives hardly touch the floorboards as we charge out the front door. All the way to the main road we steam, hearts thudding, not even daring to glance back. Another few minutes, and we're legging it down the busy road, past a parade of shops, past a pub and over to the bus stop.

'Bloody hell,' I puff when at last we reach the stop.

Dex is bent over double, wheezing like he smokes forty fags a day. He's only just got his breath back – me, too – when the bus pulls up and the doors swish open. On legs like noodles, we stagger aboard and collapse on to a seat.

Dex is the first to speak, in a whisper of total aston-ishment.

'She books an expensive holiday for one on the

day her husband is practically pronounced dead?! That's *c-o-l-d*, don't you think?'

'Yes, I do think!'

'Then the minute he comes out of his coma, she cancels it! Says she hasn't got the money she was expecting! What's that about?'

Our brains are still trying to make a jigsaw from the pieces we've got when, at last, we get to my house. It's long gone six o'clock by now and Mum is home from the salon. And fuming.

'Where have you *been*, Lozzie?' she frets as me and Dex shamble into the kitchen. 'I've called you *twice*.'

'Oh. Er, yeah, we, uh, stayed late at the theatre.'

Dex chips in eagerly, '*Twelfth Night* opens in just over a week, Mrs C.'

Mum plonks the pile of old newspapers she's holding on to the counter by the kettle and gives me her squinty-eyed look.

'Last Wednesday you said you'd rather stab yourself to death with a paperclip than set foot in a theatre again,' she says.

'Ha, ha, ha, yeah, well, er . . .' Why is no one laughing but me?

After a quarter of a century of eyeing me closely (and honestly, who can blame her?) Mum sighs.

'All right. Well, have a quick cup of tea or whatever it is you came in here for, then Dex, I want you to go home, and Loz, I want you to get on with your homework before dinner.'

Standing at the kettle, listening but not listening to Mum and Dex chattering on briefly about *Twelfth Night*, I glance at the newspaper pile. On the top is Monday's *Echo* – the one with Brian smiling up from the front page. Almost without meaning to, I start to read the main article again. And as I'm re-reading, something goes *Flash!* in my brain. I open the cupboard where we keep the tea, coffee and sugar and look inside. *Flash!* Again there's that light-burst thing in my head. By the time Mum has toddled off upstairs, my brainbox is flashing away so madly, it's like all the world's paparazzi are inside my head.

Dex starts to say something about the dosh Delilah was expecting, but I cut him off.

'Dex?'

'What?'

'How many bags of sugar do you have at home?'

'Huh?'

'How many?'

'Pff! I dunno. One, I think.'

'Same with us. There's only one at the theatre, too.'

'So?'

'So – the police found *three* bags of sugar in Brian and Delilah's house. Don't you think it weird a couple who don't eat sweet stuff and don't take sugar in their

99

tea had three big bags of sugar in their house?'

Dex frowns. 'How d'you know they don't eat sweet stuff?'

'Delilah's a diabetic – she never touches sugar; and Brian's fanatical about watching his weight. Bunty told me last week.'

Dex is now frowning so hard, if the wind changes he'll go hysterical.

'Brian took sugar in his tea, though, yeah?'

'Only a half a teaspoonful. It's not like he ladled it in.'

Dex sits back in his chair, hand to chin. You can practically hear his brainbox humming.

'Does seem weird now you mention it,' he murmurs.

Just then the Queen of Darkness, aka Karen, clomps into the kitchen and flings open the door to the fridge.

'Don't tell me you had the last Diet Coke, Big Bum,' she huffs.

'Don't tell me you're still breathing,' I snap.

'At least my arse doesn't cross postcodes,' she smirks.

'At least I'm not a swamp donkey from the realms of the undead,' I smirk back.

And to think Mum complains Karen and me never chat.

Now, normally, Dex would be giving me a secret

little smile and nodding wisely as if to say: *Swamp donkey – nice*. But this time he doesn't so much as wink. Instead he carries on thinking, thinking, and when, at last, Karen has bogged off (hallelujah), he says slowly:

'First, Delilah reveals she's expecting some big payout on Brian's death. Next, there are those unaccounted-for bags of sugar . . . Things are looking pr-e-t-t-y suspicious in her corner, don't you think?' He leans forward, elbows on table. 'I reckon we should call the police and tell them the facts we know.'

Nodding a lot, like a little kid, I reach for my moby. And stop.

'Hold on! If we tell the police what we saw and overheard at Delilah's, they might start asking questions like what were we doing in her house.'

There is a pause, then Dex thumps the table with his fist. I practically jump out of my skin.

'I'll stop off at the phone box at the end of your road and make the call from there!' he exclaims. 'That way, the police'll never trace the tip-off to me. Keep your mobile on. I'll ring you the second I'm done. OK?'

I'm up in my room still thinking about those two spare bags of uncontaminated sugar when my ringtone blares. It's Dex – so fired up, it's a minor miracle my moby doesn't melt. Turns out the policewoman who took his call was *really* interested in his tip-off . . . once she had worked out what he was saying. (To help disguise his true identity, Dex had put on his Oscar-winning French accent.)

'Did she ask your name?' I say, thinking: *Leave the French accent bit, Loz — let it lie.*

'Yeah, but it's OK – I gave her a false one.'

'What?'

Pause.

'I said my name was Dwain Dwopp.'

'Dwain Dwopp, the *French* bloke?'

'Yeah, well . . . I didn't have time to think.'

For a while longer, before Mum yells 'Dinner', Dex and me burble on about everything that's happened. We decide that even though we don't know exactly *how* or *why*, Delilah has to be in the frame for the sugar tampering.

'And to think,' I chatter, 'if we hadn't been trying to solve Ruby's disappearance we'd never have been in her house.'

'Ah . . .' Suddenly Dex sounds like he's deflating. 'Talking of Ruby . . . While I was in the phone box I saw Ed prowling up your road in his night-vision goggles, and that got me thinking . . .'

'What – it's about time the mother spaceship came and took him back?'

'It got me thinking – s'pose Ems is secretly pinning

102

her hopes on the Ace Dog Detective Agency. S'pose she hasn't yet sussed that the so-called ace detective in charge of finding Ruby is Ed.'

'Oh Nelly!' My heart sinks like a punctured rubber duck. 'She did seem suspiciously perky this morning, I forgot to tell you. She did seem a bit more like her old relaxed self.'

Dex sighs heavily. 'Which means one of us is gonna have to . . .'

'Break the truth to her gently.'

'Exactly. And congratulations, Lozzie, I nominate that person as you.'

12

The Sting's the Thing

First thing next morning, no beating about the bush, I get straight to the point with Ems.

'I know about the Ace Dog Detective Agency,' I announce.

Her toilet flushes and she comes out of the cubicle.

'Oh!' She goes over to the sinks. 'And?'

And?

'And – I don't know how to break this to you, Emsie, but the Ace Dog Detective is Dex's brother Ed.'

'I know.'

'You do?'

'Yes. I had a meeting with him yesterday. He's going to get me Ruby back.'

In the mirror I blink at her, mouth open, eyes goggling, like a cross between a startled goldfish and a bloody stunned frog.

'Ems, what are you doing? Where is your *thinking*?

Ed is not a detective! Ed is – what's the word I'm looking for? – oh yes . . . an ARSE!'

She flares, 'I know Ed's not a proper detective but at least he's come up with a plan of action, which is more than anyone else has done. The police *still* haven't traced the dognapper's moby number.'

I do not believe this. I cannot believe my ears. 'You are trusting the rescue of Ruby to Ed? *Ed!* A boy who wears a black woollen balaclava in July?'

Ems goes all huffy huff huff. 'I don't care what he wears. He's got a plan.'

'What kind of a plan?'

'A well-worked-out one.'

Bloody Nora! Not this 'well-worked-out' thing again!

By now Ems has stopped drying her hands and is heading for the door.

'So, what does this plan involve?' I ask, being remarkably reasonable.

'I'm not telling you!' she says, turning back.

'Oh!' I wasn't expecting that. 'Why?'

'Because if I tell you, you'll tell Dex, and Ed's made me promise he's not to know anything about the plan. Besides, if Dex knows, he'll tell Nat; and if Nat knows, she'll tell Tash; and if Tash knows, she'll say to me, "Just so you know, we all think you're mad."'

She's not wrong there!

At that moment Chelsea Jackson blunders into the toilets wearing a pencil skirt that's a bit unfortunate with her hips. She checks her lip-gloss in the mirror and as she leaves, Ems goes to follow her out.

'If you tell me the plan,' I say, thinking quickly, 'maybe I can help.'

There is a pause while Ems stops and has a think. Or at least I think she's having a think. It's hard to tell when all I can see is the back of her head. Turning round *finally*, she says:

'If I tell you the plan, will you swear not to repeat it to anyone, including Dex, Lee, Tash or Nat?'

'Cross my bra and hope to die.'

'Do you promise really and truly?'

'Really, truly and absolutely.'

She tells me the plan.

Crikey O'Reilly! It is so *NOT* what I was expecting to hear.

13
Dad's Brain Boots Up

'How'd she take it?' whispers Dex a few minutes later as I'm sitting down next to him for History.

'Fine,' I say, glancing anywhere except at him.

'She didn't freak out when you told her it was Ed?'

'No.'

'She wasn't gutted when she realised her ace detective is a fraud?'

'No.'

'Really? I thought she'd be destroyed.'

'No . . . well, uh, maybe a bit . . . yes, she was, a bit, but now she's like, uh, fine.'

Bloody Nora, I hate this. Lying to Dex. It feels so wrong. But hey, what can I do? I've made a promise and if I drop even a hint that there's a plan going down, he'll wheedle it out of me, just like he did after Tasha confided in me about putting those chicken fillets in her bra, and he said, 'Has Tasha got those fillet things down her bra?' and I said, 'Yes.'

Of course, just because I've resolved not to reveal the plan doesn't mean I don't think about it. Actually, I think about it A LOT. I think about it at break after me and Dex have filled the girls in on yesterday's drama. (When Dex retells the bit where I ring Delilah's phone, Nat shakes my hand and says, quite seriously, 'I feel honoured to have you for a friend.')

I think about the plan again at lunch after Lee's made me fill his best mate Barnes in on the drama, as told to him by me the night before. (When I get to the bit where I suss The Hood is Brian's decorator, Lee says to Barnes, 'Remember me tellin' you Dad's assistant Ryan found some bloke who'd collapsed after being rat-poisoned? Yeah, well, 'cause I never knew the name of that rat-poisoned bloke, it wasn't till Loz said all this last night that I learned he's that director from her elective.')

(Yeah, I *know* – who would have thought The Hood and Dave Quick's assistant Ryan are the exact same bloke?)

Anyhoo. Bizarrely, or not, I'm still thinking about the plan, sort of, when I go to visit Dad at the garage after school.

'It's my little Lozenge!' he cries, spotting me in the huge open doorway. 'Come in, come in. Mind the oil on the floor.'

Treading carefully, I cross the garage forecourt to

where he is grinning. He flings his arms wide to give me a bear hug then stops – possibly because I'm squealing, 'Overalls! Grease! No! Way!'

Dad wipes his oily hands on a clean(ish) rag.

'And to what do I owe the pleasure of this visit?' he asks.

'Nothing. Just thought I'd say hello.'

'You're not after a slice of chocolate fudge cake and a cup of tea then?'

Chocolate fudge cake? *There's chocolate fudge cake!* Whey hey!

Inside the tiny, miserable kitchen, Dad flips on the kettle and I help myself to a slice of cake from the tin. Of all the cakes in the world, chocolate fudge is my definite favourite.

If you don't count the Jaffa Cake.

Which I don't.

Because it is a biscuit.

As any muppet knows.

Tea made, cake scoffed, we go through the connecting door to the tiny, miserable office. Dad plugs in the electric fire and I sit down at the desk.

'Have you seen this?' he asks, jabbing a finger at a column of short stories in the evening edition of the *Echo*. The paper is lying open on the desk.

'D'you mean this bit: "A woman was caught stealing a frozen chicken today after hiding it under her hat and then fainting from the cold"?'

Dad roars with laughter. 'No, not that – though that is a corker. I meant the paragraph underneath.'

I read the next paragraph down.

A schoolgirl, 14, up in court this morning on a charge of driving a stolen Mini, punched her solicitor after being told she had been given a supervision order. Minutes earlier, Tonya Ravonia, who is currently suspended from school for smashing windows, had told the court: 'I've been working with groups and stuff to control my temper.'

This time both Dad *and* me howl with laughter.

Tonya Ravonia is the biggest bully on the planet – and I don't just mean she's lardy, although she is. (You wouldn't want to be standing between her and a buffet, believe me.) No, what I mean is, she's nasty and violent and totally out of control, and last term she made my life a misery – until Dad stepped in – all because, for my own private hilarity, I did a picture on the computer showing her head emerging from a horse's bum.

But that's another story.

Carrying on with this one . . . Over tea, Dad and me have one of our usual brainiac chats. He tells me about these excellent new golf balls he's bought

Uncle Nigel – they explode when you give them a thwack. How brilliant is that? And I tell him about Sunday's lunch of shame with Nana, which I had forgotten to do on Monday. I am about to mention Ruby being ransomed and leave it at that when a thought of pure genius pops into my head.

'Dad?'

'Yes?'

'If you had a pet dog that got dognapped and the police were being rubbish at finding the 'nappers, what would you do?'

'I'd come up with another way of getting the dog back.'

'Yeah, but what other way?'

'Ooh, I don't know. I'd need to think.'

'Would you, maybe, go to meet the dognapper at his chosen place, but instead of giving him real money, give him a wad of newspaper cut into the shape of bank notes with a few twenty-quid notes on top?'

Dad's face cracks into a grin. 'I like your thinking, Miss Marple! Mind you, wouldn't I be nobbled if he counted the newspaper cuttings before handing over the dog?'

'Not if you took a mate with you, and your mate was like really good at karate. He could hit the dognapper on the back of the neck while he was counting the ransom, giving you time to leg it with the dog.'

Dad leans back in his chair, arms behind his head. 'That's not a bad idea. Not bad at all. But what if there were two dognappers?'

Two dognappers?

'What if the second 'napper was able to out-sprint me and my karate chum?'

Bloody Nora! The second 'napper is a sprinter?!

Dad sits up straight. 'I'd need some back-up, don't you reckon?'

Back-up? *Back-up!* Brilliant! 'Oh yeah!'

He shoots forward in his chair.

'You know what'd be good?' he says, eyes twinkling like the lights on last year's Christmas tree before they fused the house.

'What?'

'If there was a group of people hiding in cars around the handover point. As the dognapper pre-pared to count the ransom, they could all rush for-wards shouting, "Police, Police," and wrestle both 'nappers to the ground. That way the villains would get caught and the dog would be returned. A result all round.'

I look at Dad in complete and total admiration.

'That's genius, Dad! Excellent. Wait till I tell Ems!'

His eyes go like slits. 'Ems? Why Ems?'

'Er, no reason.'

Pause.

'Are you up to something, Lauren?'

'No! 'Course not! What makes you say that?'

'Because you usually are.'

Fair point.

'Well, I'm not up to anything, OK?'

'OK. So, why are you anxious to tell Emma all this?'

'I'm not! It's just . . .'

One of Dad's eyebrows goes up. 'It's just what?'

'It's just . . . Oh, all right, all right. It's just Emsie's dog Ruby has been stolen, yeah? And me and her were thinking of things we, er, people could do, people like, uh, her dad could do to get Ruby back.'

My armpits are now sweating, which is delightful. Dad seems to be thinking hard.

'I see,' he says slowly, nodding wisely. Then: 'Is this the sort of thing you often think about, Loz – scams and stings and the like?'

I shrug. 'Yeah. Sometimes. Occasionally.' (Hardly ever.)

He grins. 'I had no idea. What a chip off the old block! Tell Emma if her dad wants an extra man, I'm in!'

★ ★ ★

Thursday is Mum's night at salsa with her mate Man-Mad Marge (main hobbies: smoking fags and drinking gin). Thursday is also the night Morticia does waitressing at Pizza Heaven. I wait for the two of them to dolly themselves up and troll off, then dash downstairs to phone Ems. I have to use the landline in the hallway because Mum is threatening to stop topping up my moby if I don't cut down on my calls.

I begin, 'Ems. Hi. Me. Listen, about Operation Ruby.' And before she can say, 'Hello, who is this?' I tell her all about the possibility of a second dognapper who may or may not be an Olympic sprinter, and about the vital, urgent need for a back-up unit.

'But we're going to need at least one adult for the hiding in cars bit,' she says. 'Where're we going to find an adult with a car who won't go mental parental when we tell them what we're doing? We don't have much time to sort this, Loz. The handover is only in two days.'

The handover with the dognapper has been set for one o'clock on Saturday afternoon on the patch of wasteland between the bus depot and the rec.

I say, 'Look, how about I get my dad to help?'

All at once, Ems has a fit of such biblical proportions I wonder if she shouldn't be airlifted to hospital. 'Oh no, no. Oh God, Loz, no. Don't mention this to your dad, *please*, I beg.'

Oops. 'He'd be cool about it,' I promise. 'Really.'

'It's not that. It's just your dad fixes my dad's car, yeah, and if he let slip about the plan to my dad, my dad would kill me. More than once.'

She has a point. Of all the stern, strict dads ever to be stern and strict, Mr Hodgson is the sternest. And the strictest. Once, when I was round their house for lunch — the kind of lunch where everyone sits nicely at the dining-room table and no one empties condoms out of their bag — Mrs Hodgson said, 'Would you like some prawns, Lauren?' and getting my tongue in a twist, I said, 'Yes, please, I love porn,' and Ems's dad glared at me. For like an hour!

'OK, OK, I won't ask Dad.' From Emsie's end of the line there's a whoosh of relief. 'I'll find someone else. Leave that to me.'

Already my brain is Action-Stations-Go. Here's what I'm thinking: if I can get Hattie to help and she brings her girlfriend Megan, that's two adults, plus a camper van, plus me, plus Dex, which is a mobile surveillance back-up unit — sort of.

I carry on, 'The crucial thing now is to make Ed see how Operation Ruby needs proper back-up if we are to catch the dognapper, and to tell him you want me and Dex to be in on the sting.'

Ems leaps on that. 'Oh no, Loz, no. He'll never accept the Dex bit.'

'Tell him it's either that or you're calling the whole plan off!'

Ems squeals like a scaredy kitten. Oh dear. Time for a quick rethink.

'OK, well, maybe don't put it as harsh as that,' I say. 'Maybe just tell him we all reckon his plan is genius and we don't want to muscle in on it big-time or anything, we only want to be there in the background as security, just in case. Tell him he'll still get his karate moment, he'll still be the one in charge.'

'OK,' says Ems, kind of thoughtfully, after a bit. 'I reckon he might go along with that if I make it clear everyone knows he's the boss. Besides, it's not like he's the *only* one with a say in Operation Ruby, is it? I mean, *I'm* the one paying for it.'

There is a pause.

'You are paying Ed a *fee*?'

''Course. Have to. I signed a contract.'

'*Contract?* You've got a contract, too?'

'This is business, Lozzie! What d'you expect?'

Holy Moley!

Am I the only person I know who's not on pills?

★ ★ ★

After Businesswoman of the Year has got off the phone, I call Hat and fill her in on Operation Ruby, and tell her how really, really grateful me and Ems would be if she and Megan would burst out of the camper pretending to be undercover cops.

All the time I'm gabbing away, she just listens patiently. Then at last she says, 'Of course I'll help get Ruby back. I'd be glad to. Dognappers are such heartless bastards. It'd be great to be able to put at least one of them out of business.'

Now, I didn't know this before, I only find it out during our chat, but Eric was nearly dognapped once. Apparently, not long ago, Hattie tied him to a railing outside a shop and when she came back she saw some bloke pulling him up the street. She stormed up to the bloke and said, 'What are you doing with my dog?' and he said he'd spotted Eric wandering about with his lead trailing and thought he was lost.

Hat carries on, 'Of course it's possible Eric could have slipped his lead and wandered off; the man was incredibly charming. But still, I have my doubts.'

It's nearly nine o'clock when Hattie and me get off the phone. By now I am going out of my mind with starvation, so it's Kitchen-Here-I-Come! Mum has been banging on at Morticia and me lately about the importance of eating sensibly, *soooo* for starters, I have the rest of yesterday's leftover feta cheese salad. Chomp chomp, chew chew, virtue. And for main course, I have a packet of salt 'n' vinegar crisps dipped in salad cream. Yum yum, bubble gum. It was Dex who first introduced me to the very excellent *crisps à la salad crème*. He got the recipe from his granddad. Dex's granddad is lovely. Once he gave me and Dex a tenner for absolutely no reason at all.

So . . . there I am sitting at the kitchen table, dunking crisps in salad cream, thinking some quite interesting thoughts, when what happens? My moby rings. Quick as a wotsit, I scoot up to my room to answer it, and hurrah, hooray! Lee's name is on the screen. I press the button, ready to gabble, 'Hey, sweetie!' when suddenly a shockwave shudders through my veins. Down the line I can hear the faraway sound of a girl laughing. Squeakily. Fast as a flash, I re-check the display. It is Lee's number for definite. His phone must have dialled mine by mistake. I flatten the moby to my head. This time there are other noises. Background noises. Like rustling. And murmuring. And . . . it *can't* be . . . it *is.* It's *kissing.* He's kissing. Lee's *kissing* Felicity. Now he's saying something. He's saying, 'C'mon, baby. You know you want to.'

My heart stops.

My stomach knots.

Oh God, I think I'm going to be sick.

14
The Big Betrayal

I am still in my bedroom, hunched on the bed, when Mum comes home. My face must have gone grey or something, because when she pops her head round the door she says, 'What's the matter?'

I open my mouth to tell her but nothing comes out. I try again but the sounds are all stuttery, jagged like broken glass. Mum hurries over and wraps me up in her arms. And that's when the tears pour down my cheeks, like an unstoppable flood.

'I-i-t's Lee,' I stammer, gulping air in between sobs.

'What about him? Is he hurt?'

'Worse.'

'How worse?'

'H-h-he's seeing someone else.'

'Oh, love.'

And out it comes, the whole horrid, horrible story of the nasty overheard call. With one arm around my shoulders, Mum waits till I've stopped sobbing and shuddering, and then she starts softly to talk. She tells me being betrayed is never easy and I must wait till the shock's worn off before talking to Lee. She also tells me how it's important to remember that boys like him are ten a penny but I am special – precious and loyal, funny and brave, and she and Dad love me very much.

Well, that does it. That sets me off sobbing and shuddering all over again. By the time I've got a grip and straightened up, finally, at last, there are enough crumpled-up tissues on the floor to carpet a small hall.

After a bit, Mum makes us both a hot chocolate, then runs me a bath. If she's noticed the empty crisp packet and bottle of salad cream on the kitchen table, she doesn't let on. Even Morticia is remarkably sympathetic (for her) when she gets in. OK, so at first she says, 'What's wrong with your eyes? If you've got that eye infection Nana had, don't nick my mascara and pass it on to me.' But once Mum's explained that I have been crying over Lee, she says some quite nice stuff.

Later that night, long after the rest of the house has gone to sleep, I lie in bed and think about Lee. And the more I think, the more the pieces of the devastating puzzle fit together in my head. Of course Felicity hadn't been looking to cop off with Darren at the football: she'd been there to snare Lee! No wonder her and Man Hands had been giving me the superior eye in the bowling alley. And when Lee said he'd had to help his dad on Sunday because his dad's assistant Ryan never works Sundays, that was a lie. Of course his dad's assistant works Sundays. That's the day he went round to Delilah's and found Brian nearly dead. Why would Lee lie about something like that unless he'd been somewhere he shouldn't have been – i.e. with Felicity?

When you're staring up at the ceiling, heart emptied out, it's hard not to think there's nothing left worth living for any more. Apart from Mum and Dad . . . and my nanas and Granddad . . . and Dex, Ems, Nat and Tash . . . Possibly Orlando Bloom. Definitely James Franco from *Spider-Man 3*. Ditto that bloke on the Galaxy chocolate commercial. Ooh, and Peter Kay, because he's well funny. And *Morecambe and Wise* repeats on the TV. And *Reeves and Mortimer*. And . . . zzzzzzzzzzzzzzz.

* * *

Dex is already at the bus stop when I trudge up next morning.

'Guess what!' he bubbles excitedly. 'I've got ne –' He stops and squints at my face like a doctor examining a patient. 'What's up with your eyes? Have you been crying?'

Sucking in a deep breath, I fill him in on the dismal tragedy that is my love life. All the while I'm talking his face looks more angry than shocked. When I get to the bit of the overheard call where Lee says, 'C'mon, baby, you know you want to,' he erupts,

'Oh, *perl-e-a-se*! That idiot is such a *player*!' There is a silence for a bit. Then: 'You know what? Miserable though all this is, in a way Lee's done you a favour.'

'How do you work that one out?'

'Well, you two would've split up eventually. This way, you can move on quickly and find someone better, someone more special, someone more suited to you.'

'What d'you mean, we would have split up any-way? Who says?'

'It stands to reason. Lee's outstandingly buff an' all that, but he's not exactly a laugh, is he? He's not funny or chatty or original. He's not even interested in anything except football . . . oh, and himself. Sooner or later you'd have stopped being so caught up in the thrill of having your first serious boyfriend and you'd've noticed. Then you'd have dumped him.'

I am shook to my core. Truly. More than if I'd just been slapped round the chops with a haddock.

'You're being very mature and wise about this,' I say, after a bit.

'I have always been mature and wise,' he replies breezily. 'It is one of the many burdens I'm forced to bear.'

Just then the bus pulls up and the Dalai Lama and me get on board. As we're plonking ourselves down at the back, I say:

'So, what's this news you were gonna tell me?'

If this were a pantomime Dex would be rubbing his hands together with glee.

'The police have taken Delilah in for questioning,' he says.

'Woo!'

'I know! This morning's *Echo* said she is helping them with their enquiries following an anonymous tip-off!'

'Whey hey!'

A few high-fives and a load of grinning later, me and Dex get into school. All the girls are waiting for us in the grounds, hanging back a bit from the main gate. On MSN the night before, I had poured out my hurt to them, big-time. It was like being online with three different versions of Dr Pru, *Rebel*'s love guru. Tasha wrote: *Txt him, he's ova, end of.* Nat put: *Tell him he's dumped, but face 2 face.* Ems, being Ems, went: *Mayb he's sorry. Tlk it thru. C wot he has 2 say.*

For reasons I can only put down to temporary insanity, I decide to take the advice of Ems. Don't ask me why – she knows less about this love stuff than I do. When it comes to boyfriends the record is:

Me: 1
Nat: 0
Tash: 5
Ems: 0

Anyhoo. Inside the main gate, the girls rally round.

Ems says, 'Lee's not in yet and Felicity's at the doctor's.'

'With malaria, we're hoping.' This is Tash.

At that very moment Nat gives me the kind of nudge that could crack a rib; and turning round, I see Lee sauntering through the gate. Tash whispers, 'Go, girl! Go girl!' And over I march to meet him.

'Hey, babe,' he begins. 'What's –?'

'I know about you and Felicity Bagnall.'

There is a pause.

'I-I dunno what you're on about.'

'Yes, you do.'

'No, I don't.'

My insides really snarl up. How can he *lie* about this?

I suck in a deep breath. 'OK, if you're not seeing Felicity, how come yesterday you two were . . . you know . . . doing it?'

His face goes shrimp pink; his eyes flick from side to side like he's about to do a runner.

'What you on about?' He's looking at his feet now. 'We weren't doin' nothin'. Babe, c'mon. You're stressin' over nothin'.'

He puts his arm round my shoulders and squeezes me all matey-like.

'If you weren't doing anything yesterday, how come when your phone rang mine by mistake I heard you smooching, "C'mon, baby, you know you want to"?'

Honestly, he lets go of me so flick-knife quick, I almost let out a gasp.

'What is this?' he flares. 'You checkin' up on me? You stalking me? What are you, some kinda stalker?'

Stalker? *Stalker!* HOW DARE HE? How dare he try to blame this on me!

'I don't need this right now,' he blusters. 'I don't need this. Me an' you was supposed to be about havin' a laugh.'

And just like that he storms into school, bag bouncing against his back – first bell long gone.

Fizzing, absolutely *fizzing,* with fury, I storm inside too. I'm so mad I could head-butt a wall. Two walls. And a door. If anyone makes eye contact with me, I will kill them. Truly.

All through double French I sit rigid with rage. At

break when I tell the others what Lee had said, Ems's eyes jam open so wide, you'd think someone had given her a wedgie. Tasha steams like a boiling kettle.

'You have *sooo* got to get back at him for this,' she cries. 'He is *sooo* out of order. Let's slash the tyres on his bike. Let's tell everyone he's a crap kisser.'

Nat cruises in. 'Tyre slashing's not the way to go. It's too . . . what's the word . . . psycho.' She produces a small packet of Hobnobs from up her sleeve and passes them round. 'What we need, my cheery chums, is a plan of revenge. A plan that'll make it hard for Lee to uphold his reputation. A plan that will make him look a total wassock in front of his mates. What d'you think?'

We all think this is *exactly* the way to go. But as it turns out, there's no need for any of us to come up with a plan because, although we don't know it at the time, Operation Ruby is about to take care of that.

15
Operation Ruby

If Operation Ruby were a Hollywood film, the cast of *Ocean's Thirteen* would NOT be in it. When Hattie and Megan pull up on Marine Drive to collect us, Ems is panicking and Ed is in disguise: as what, it's hard to say – he's got on his dad's Elvis wig and an anorak. And when we look in the back of the camper, Bunty is sitting there with a cycle helmet on her head and a travel rug over her knees. Ems takes one look at this, the final member of our crack surveillance unit, and her face goes paper white.

Big smiles all round, Bunty opens the back of the van and me, Dex, Ems and Elvis clamber in; Hat and Megan are up front. Just so you know, it's been decided Ed and Megan, not Ed and Ems, will be making the exchange with the dognapper at the wasteland because:

1. The dognapper might get suspicious if two kids turn up alone; and

2. Megan is a docker of a girl who knows how to kickbox.

The introductions stuff done, Ed slaps on his tough-guy face and stares at each of us in turn. Then slowly, and without any expression in his voice (what's new?), he says:

'At thirteen hundred hours the fox will enter the henhouse and the exchange will be made. This is a highly dangerous fit-up, but there's no need to panic – me and Megan have been trained. At my signal you will exit the vehicle and approach the perp in a SWAT team manner. If he is uncooperative and fails to surrender, I will punch him in the gob. If he is still uncooperative and fails to surrender, Megan will kick him in the goolies. Are there any questions?'

There are no questions, obviously, because it is clear Ed is an arse. And much, much later, after the whole sting is over, Bunty says:

'Did anyone understand what the little lad was saying? Or why he was in fancy dress?'

★ ★ ★

The waste ground is at the top of Wilson Avenue, next to the bus depot on one side and a recreation ground on the other. When we get there it is deserted. Totally. Scraggly bushes, heaps of junk, a few beat-up old cars (four of them in a row at right angles to the depot) – that's it. Megan parks the camper parallel to the row of cars, about fifty metres away from it. Then Ed and Hattie get out and swap places so that he and Megan are up front. The rest of us do as we're told by Ed and crouch low in the back underneath the van's long windows, ears straining, listening out for the sound of the dognapper's van.

'Would any one like a scone?' 'whispers' Bunty after a bit, pulling a Tupperware box out from under her rug.

'Ooh, yes please,' we all squeak, except for Ed, who scowls darkly, and Ems, who is too bunched up with worry to eat.

Bunty hands round the scones and Dex, Hattie, Megan and me pounce on them like a starving ship-wrecked crew.

We've been on covert surveillance for exactly five minutes.

'They were delicious, Bunty,' Megan says, after we've scoffed the lot. 'Shame you've got no more. I'm starving.'

Ed says flatly, 'If you were starving, Megan, really starving, you'd boil your shoes and eat those.'

'Oh, don't be a silly, Ed,' chuckles Bunty. 'You can't eat accessories. Accessories aren't food.'

Ed again: 'If you were starving, Megan, you'd eat

your shoes. That's if you hadn't eaten one of us first.'

Just then there's the sound of a vehicle bouncing over bumpy ground. Thank God. Instantly, Ed and Megan get out of the camper, and the rest of us bob our heads up and peek out of the window. Up ahead, a white van is rolling to a stop near the last beat-up car in the row. Ed and Megan walk over to it quickly. The driver's and passenger's doors both open. Two men in black clothes get out. One is taller and thinner than the other. Both are wearing balaclavas. Hat signals like mad for us to duck. We duck.

'OK,' she breathes slowly, her eyes glued to the glass. 'This is it.'

My heart goes thump.

'One of the dognappers is opening the back of the van.'

I shoot Ems a shaky smile.

'Ruby is out . . .'

My stomach makes like a fist.

'Ready . . .'

I hold my breath.

'Steady . . .'

I'm still holding my breath.

'GO!'

Like frantic frogs in a burning box we all leap madly in the direction of the door; Ems is practically flattened by Bunty. Then Hattie blurts, 'NO!' and we freeze and stare out of the window, eyes on stalks. A bus is speeding across the depot's car park and ripping straight through its wooden barrier – *smash!* It ploughs into the line of beat-up old cars – *crash!* The cars flip on to one another – *thud, thud, thud!* The thudding jolts open the back doors of the dognappers' white van – *bang!* And out streams a pack of dogs. The noise is ear-shattering, worse than a riot: dogs barking, bus horns blaring, people running out of the depot yelling – the works.

Above the racket Hattie shouts, 'GO, GO, GO,' and out of the camper we charge . . . straight into the path of the fleeing dognappers. They take one glance at Cycle Helmet Woman and the rest of the Scooby Doo crew, and dart to their right. Too slow! With a war cry so loud you'd have to be dead and buried under a paving slab not to hear it, Bunty launches herself on to the shorter 'napper's back, and he hits the ground, *ouf*, like a sack of wet cement. Using all her weight, she pins his thrashing arms to his sides and Hattie jumps on his legs.

Yeeeesssss!

Superb!

Thunderbird Girls Are Go!

Meanwhile . . .

The second dognapper is haring away, chased by Ed, Megan, Dex and all the yapping dogs freed from the van. Shooting Ems a quick look – she's too busy hugging Ruby to see – I put my size fives into gear and dash off after them. As I'm running, I glance behind me at the bolted bus . . . and my eyebrows practically hit a plane overhead. There, legging it away from the busted-up cab, is Tonya Ravonia.

Behind her, in furious pursuit, every bus inspector on the planet.

The second dognapper is in top nick, fitness-wise, I'll give him that. He steams ahead at full speed. Panting like mad, pant pant, pant pant, I keep him and the others in sight as he tears across the wasteland and over the road to the rec. There's a football match going on on the grass, but that doesn't stop our chase. The 'napper flies straight through the game, down the centre line, and all the players stop dead in their tracks.

All except one.

All except Lee.

The moment he sees the pack of barking dogs streaming towards him, he spins on his heels and runs like a demented chicken. His footie mates howl, the spectators roar, and Felicity Bagnall, who is standing pitch-side, makes a face like she's just laid a very large egg.

Happy days!

But no time to linger, no time to linger – the dognapper is getting away. And fast. By now I'm sweating like a boxer; my shirt is stuck to my back, but still I keep on running, along with the four dogs that aren't after Lee, and the rest of the Scooby Doo crew. The 'napper must be sweating buckets as well because as he nears the edge of the rec he yanks off his balaclava and chucks it aside.

'We're losing him,' shouts Ed as the fleeing figure crosses the rec's car park. For the first time the 'napper glances over his shoulder to see how close behind we are, then darts like a raving lunatic across the busy road.

'*Damn*,' puffs Megan, coming to a stop on the wrong side of the tarmac and grabbing two of the dogs to stop them. Ed grabs the third dog; Dex the fourth. There's *way* too much traffic for any of us to risk weaving through it.

'If only we'd seen where he went,' wheezes Megan, trying to catch her breath. 'If only we knew his name.'

But here's the thing: we *do* know his name. Or at least me and Dex do, because when he glanced backwards, we saw his face.

It was the face of Ryan Bentley.

Aka Dave Quick's assistant.

Aka The Hood.

But that's not the only shock in the shock store cupboard. No way, José! When we get back to the camper, legs like rubber, the police have arrived, and they're bundling the first 'napper into a black maria.

Which is detective slang for a police car.

Which means I am now talking like Ed.

Good grief!

As a policeman is ordering the unmasked dognapper into the car, Hattie gabbles:

'He's the man I was telling you about, Loz. The one I caught trying to drag Eric along. The one who claimed he had slipped his lead.'

I go over to the police car and look at the man's face through the wound-up window. And as I'm looking, slowly, slowly something starts to make sense in my brain. No wonder Eric had burst out barking so berserkly that afternoon on the beach: he had recognised the dognapper who had tried to abduct him; he had recognised the man now under arrest; he had recognised . . . Dave Quick.

16

Sugar and Spite and Opening Night

After Dave Quick has been driven away, and the dogs have been rounded up, and a photographer from the *Echo* has snapped our picture, the Scooby Doo crew goes back to Hattie's for a massive celebration. On the ride over we sing 'We Are the Champions' by Queen; Ruby howls throughout and Ems looks happy enough to burst. When we get indoors, Megan whops on 'Jailhouse Rock' by Elvis as a tribute to Ed's wig and everyone does mad rock 'n' roll dancing. Even Eric and Ruby dash around, trying to join in the fun until the Loopy One knocks over a table and Hattie shoos them outdoors.

'I'd like to propose a toast,' says Hat, raising her glass, after everyone's been given something fizzy to drink. 'To Squad Operation Ruby, the best undercover surveillance operatives in the business.'

We all chink glasses, grinning like numpties on an awayday. Then Ems gives an emotional thank-you speech, which makes us girls well up. And Megan proposes a round of applause for Ed because it was his plan.

'Check out our team leader,' I whisper to Dex as Ed stands in the centre of the room, smiling bashfully, lapping up the clapping. 'He's so loving this, you could set fire to his wig and he wouldn't notice.'

Dex grunts sourly, 'It's all right for you. You're not the one who's never gonna hear the end of how he apprehended a perp.'

I give him a squeeze. 'You can always tell him to shut up and if he's uncooperative and fails to surrender, sit on his head.'

Dex grins, and from that moment on, one of us only has to say, 'This is a dangerous fit-up, but don't panic, I have been trained,' and we're laughing like loons.

★ ★ ★

Brilliantly, Operation Ruby makes front-page news in Monday's *Echo*. The headline announces to the world:

DOGNAPPING DUO BUSTED BY HAVE-A-GO-HEROES

The article underneath mentions that Dave Quick and The Hood have been charged with theft, which means, according to Mum, they'll probably be fined and get a suspended prison sentence. Alongside the article there's a photograph of the Scooby Doo crew, with Ed in the middle, arms folded, face mean.

Mum bursts out laughing when she sees Ed in his tough-guy pose.

'Don't forget to show that to Dad when next you see him,' she says.

After I had got home on Saturday, I had told Mum all about Operation Ruby. I hadn't intended to – well, not straight after getting in so late. But once I had said I'd been round at Hattie's, she said, 'What were you doing at Hattie's?' and I said, 'Celebrating,' and she said, 'Celebrating what?' and next thing you know, I was singing like a canary.

Which is detective slang for 'giving evidence like a police informer'.

Which means I'm doing it *again* – talking like Ed.

I may have to be put down.

Anyhoo. Mercifully, Mum didn't immediately ground me for eternity for impersonating an under-cover cop. Thank Nelly. Instead she said she was extremely proud of me for being such a good friend to Ems, but if ever I did anything as dangerous as that again I would be in BIG trouble. Then I said, 'You don't seem very stunned about Dave Quick being a dognapper, Mum,' and she replied, 'Oh no, I am

shocked. Of course I am. I would never have suspect-
ed him of committing a crime. It's just . . . well,
towards the end of our relationship, I caught a glimpse
of the man beneath the good looks and the easy
charm, and he wasn't a warm, kind man. That's all.'

Now, you don't need to be Mystic Meg to know
Operation Ruby is major news at school on Monday,
too. Frank Fabiola comes up to me before first bell
and says, 'I heard one of the dognappers pulled a gun
on you.'

I go, 'Er, no.'

Rocco Ramero comes up to Dex and says, 'I heard
you beat one of the 'nappers to a pulp.'

Dex goes, 'Er, yes. Yes, I did.'

All through break I keep my beadies peeled for Lee
– to check how he's taking his dad's arrest – but he's
nowhere about. In the cafeteria at lunchtime, I ask
Barnes where he is and he says he's called in sick.

'Probably just as well,' says Ems kindly as me and
the girls sit down to share a couple of bowls of cheesy
pasta.

She has a point. Today would not have been a good
day for Lee to be in, what with one half of the school
gossiping about his dad, and the other half laughing
about him being a big girl's blouse who's afraid of
dogs.

'I do feel kinda bad about the thing with his dad,' I

say, stabbing a bit of pasta on to my fork. 'Lee hadn't the faintest foggiest what he was up to.'

According to Barnes, who has spoken to Lee, Dave Quick always kept the stolen dogs out of sight, in his lock-up.

'Yeah, all this is tough on Lee,' says Tash, nodding sympathetically. Then, leaning forward intently, she adds: 'Show us again that expression on Felicity's face when it looked like she was laying an egg.'

As predicted by Dex and me, Dave Quick is not the only criminal to be seriously exposed in the *Echo*. When we get to the theatre on Wednesday, the building is buzzing with the latest breaking story: Delilah has been charged with attempted murder by product-tampering.

'I can't believe it,' flusters Bunty in the kitchen. She's fishing a teabag out of a cup, I'm refilling the kettle (*quelle surprise*) and Dex is glancing at a copy of the *Echo* spread open on the table. 'I knew the police had taken her in for questioning but I thought that was simply routine. She said that was simply routine. But to be charged? To be actually *charged* with attempted murder! How could she do such a dreadful thing? How could she want her own husband dead?'

Dex shoots me a look that says: *Did she not meet him?* I squelch a grin and, teacup in hand, Bunty flurries out the door.

No sooner has she gone than the two of us pounce on the paper on the table. The story of Delilah's arrest is all over the front page and most of the inside pages, too. According to the main article, Delilah is claiming she's totally innocent and the police have made a massive mistake, but as Dex says, 'It's obvious it's a fair cop.' And he's not wrong about that.

For a start, it turns out in the year leading up to the sugar-tampering, Delilah had taken out *three* life insurance policies in Brian's name and forged his signature on all of them. The policies guaranteed to pay her half a million quid if Brian died accidentally, and under the terms of the policies, death by product-tampering counts as accidental death.

'So *that* was the big payout Delilah had been expecting,' Dex says, more to himself than to me.

And another thing: when the police checked local libraries, they found Delilah's fingerprints on two reference books about poisons. And the biggest concentration of those prints was on the pages about Trithium.

'Does it mention the two extra bags of non-poisoned sugar she had at home?' I ask, going over to the cupboard to get out the teabags. The kettle has clicked itself off, and I am, as usual, under orders to make tea for the whole of Britain.

'I'm just looking,' mumbles Dex, reading the rest of

the article. 'Ah! Found it. This is it: "Early on in the investigation Mrs Archer was asked why she had three large bags of sugar in her cupboard. She replied that her husband had a very sweet tooth; however, following an anonymous tip-off from a member of the public, the police have found this not to be true."'

I pat Dex on the back. 'Whey hey!'

He grins. 'You know what I think,' he says, folding up the paper. 'I think the two uncontaminated bags were there as back-up.'

'How d'you mean?'

'I reckon Delilah poisoned seven bags – one to leave in her cupboard for Brian to use, and six to be sneaked back on to shop shelves. She probably thought: *If no one gets struck down quickly, I can poison the two spare bags and slip them into shops to hurry things up.* After all, she only needed one person to get sick or die before she could poison Brian and have the police declare a product-tampering scare.'

For a moment I look at Dex in complete wonder and amazement. Sometimes it's easy to forget that the part of his brain that deals with brilliant thoughts and very brainy stuff really is gobsmackingly big.

It's about now that Hattie pops her head round the door, in a total tizz, to tell us to get a wiggle on because the dress rehearsal is about to begin.

Three days later, she's popping her head round the

kitchen door again, in even more of a tizz, to tell us to get a wiggle on because the opening performance is about to start.

And what a bloody performance it is.

First up, rumour has it Brian will be in the front row of the audience, which sends all the actors into a nervous-nelly spin. Then, half an hour before curtain-up, someone twigs that Lionel, who plays Sir Andrew Aguecheek, is drunk, so the cast hold an emergency summit meeting and decide to do the show without him. Which means in one scene Olive, who plays Viola, has a sword fight with thin air, and in another scene Bunty, who plays Maria, has this conversation with herself:

Maria Now, sir, thought is free.

Silence while we all wait for Sir Andrew's reply, which naturally doesn't come.

Maria It's dry, sir.

More silence while Maria waits for Sir Andrew's hilarious wisecrack.

Maria Ha ha ha ha ha ha ha.

More silence.

Maria Ha ha ha ha ha.

Lord alone knows what the audience think is going on. To any sane person, it must seem like Maria has suddenly been struck with Mad Cow Disease.

Mind you, things aren't any less crackers backstage. In fact, it's like pandemonium gone mad behind the scenes. Dex has to keep running back and forth behind the scenery, reading out Olive's lines because she's forgotten most of them. And because there's no Delilah, I have to dash about helping the actors with their costume changes.

Which means I have to get Desmond into his thong.

Which means I shall probably need psychiatric care for life.

Do these people not know I am only *fourteen*!

Only once in the whole show do I have a laugh – when Dex, as bystander-in-the-street, plonks himself centre-stage and runs through every facial expression known to humanity. By the time the curtain comes down, most of the audience practically have to be sedated, they are laughing so much. Brian is crying. Actual tears!

'You do know Brian is whimpering, don't you?' I say to Dex, standing beside him in the wings.

'That's the magic of *Twelfth Night*,' he replies straight-facedly.

Holy Moley.

Good grief!